THE MOST WANTED WOMEN IN THE WEST!

Some were great beauties, others often disguised themselves as men. Some acted as spies and go-betweens for outlaw gangs, others stood ready to kill any man who got in their way. Some became famous for their courage and skill, others made their notoriety pay off in a big way.

One and all, they were a breed apart, not content to stay quietly at home, cooking and cleaning and raising kids. They wanted more out of life—excitement, money, and fame. And they found what they were looking for when they became the—

WILD WOMEN
OF THE WEST

Ⓢ SIGNET BRAND WESTERN

D1164361

MENTOR Anthologies You'll Want to Read

WILD WOMEN OF THE WEST

Carl W. Breihan

A SIGNET BOOK

NEW AMERICAN LIBRARY

TIMES MIRROR

Copyright © 1982 by Carl W. Breihan

 SIGNET TRADEMARK REG. U.S. PAT. OFF. AND FOREIGN COUNTRIES
REGISTERED TRADEMARK—MARCA REGISTRADA
HECHO EN CHICAGO, U.S.A.

SIGNET, SIGNET CLASSICS, MENTOR, PLUME, MERIDIAN AND NAL BOOKS
are published by The New American Library, Inc.,
1633 Broadway, New York, New York 10019

First Printing, November, 1982

1 2 3 4 5 6 7 8 9

PRINTED IN THE UNITED STATES OF AMERICA

414   (1982-83)

To John Wayne,
a good friend
who is sorely missed

Contents

1.

Laura Bullion, Alias Della Rose

Of all the women connected with the Wild Bunch of outlaws, Laura Bullion has remained the most misunderstood. Though perhaps not as "mysterious" as the beautiful Etta Place, Laura Bullion's life has nevertheless been shrouded in mystery, and her origins have never been known, until now. The veil of mystery has recently been lifted, and the life—and death—of this wild and woolly woman of the West can at last be told.

Laura Bullion was born about 1876 on the ranch of her father, James Scott, near Knickerbocker, Texas. But in a sense Laura was not the daughter of Jim Scott, and herein lies the incredible story of her origin.

James Scott had married Elizabeth Lambert and shortly thereafter had settled on his ranch near Knickerbocker. Scott was an itinerant livestock dealer and was frequently away from home, leaving his new bride alone to care for the chores of the ranch.

On one such absence Elizabeth Scott suffered a terrible ordeal when she was captured by a band of Comanche Indians and was raped. Scott could never forgive his wife for the event, in some way blaming her for the entire thing, especially when she discovered that she was pregnant by one of the Comanches. Scott abandoned his

1

wife, who soon thereafter gave birth to a daughter she named Laura.

Elizabeth Scott was left with no resources to care for her young daughter, and so, when Laura was still very young, she was given over to the care of a neighbor woman, Mrs. Bullion, to be raised. Mrs. Bullion was the widow of a German immigrant named Eduoard Bullion, and had at least one other child, Edward Bullion. In later years, Ed Bullion joined the Blackjack Ketchum gang under the alias of Ed Cullen, his mother's maiden name. Elizabeth Lambert Scott later married a man named Byler.

By the age of twelve, Laura was living with the Bullions on a sheep ranch in Concho County, Texas. She accompanied the cowboys onto the range and rode a horse bareback, Comanche style. She could rope and shoot as well as any man.

About 1890, handsome young Will Carver entered the scene. He was a dashing young outlaw recently arrived from Utah and Wyoming, and he was an associate of Blackjack Tom Ketchum and the Kilpatricks, and the teenaged Laura immediately fell in love with him.

Although the love affair with Carver continued over a period of years in sporadic fashion, Laura lost her heart when Carver introduced her to his friend Ben Kilpatrick, the Tall Texan. The story that Carver lost Laura to Kilpatrick in a poker game probably has no basis in fact.

In 1895 Ben Kilpatrick and Laura were together at Brown's Park, the outlaw stronghold on the border of Utah-Wyoming-Colorado, posing as man and wife. If they were ever legally married, the record has never been found.

Meanwhile, Ed Bullion—alias Edwin Cullen, alias Edward H. Cullen, alias John A. Hespatch, et al., adoptive brother of Laura Bullion—was maintaining a reputation as a member of the Blackjack Ketchum gang.

At about the time Laura and Ben Kilpatrick went to Brown's Park, Ed Bullion left Colorado City, Texas, and appeared in Cochise County, Arizona, where he took employment for several years as a range cook with the San Simon Cattle Company and later with the Erie Cattle Company.

In the latter part of November 1897, Ed Bullion was unemployed and left the camp of Erie foreman Sam Hayhurst south of Bisbee and joined the Ketchum gang in Texas Canyon.

On the evening of December 9, 1897, Ed Bullion and Dave Atkins robbed the post office and the Wells Fargo Express agent St. John at Stein's Pass, New Mexico, near the Arizona border, obtaining a total of $11.20 for their efforts, and then joined Sam Ketchum and awaited a signal from Tom Ketchum and Will Carver, who were cutting the telegraph line outside of town, near the railroad track.

As train Number 20 rolled up the grade and approached Stein's station, Sam Ketchum, Atkins, and Bullion forced St. John to post a red light at the depot to stop the train. The train halted and conductor Russell and a brakeman stepped down and entered the office to be confronted by the outlaws' guns. In the express car were messenger Charles J. Adair and guards C. H. Jennings and Eugene Thacker.

The three outlaws at the depot boarded the train and compelled engineer Tom North to pull the train outside of town and stop between two bonfires on the track, where waited Tom Ketchum and Will Carver.

The defenders of the express car refused to open the door, but instead set up a barrage of shotgun fire which lasted more than half an hour. Then, at 9:15 P.M., Ed Bullion became careless and leaned forward from his position behind the express car to reach for extra cartridges, and Jennings literally blew a hole in Bullion's head with his shotgun. "Boys, I am dead!" he screamed to his companions, who quickly mounted and rode away. Prophetically, Ed Bullion was dead within seconds and his body was loaded aboard the train and taken to Lordsburg, New Mexico, for an inquest. Laura's adoptive brother was now dead, but Laura Bullion, alias Della Rose, was still riding the outlaw trail.

Although there were certainly others, Laura Bullion participated in at least one major robbery with the Wild Bunch, the last major robbery of Butch Cassidy in the United States.

The target chosen was the Great Northern train near Exeter, Montana. Cassidy, who masterminded the job, chose Ben Kilpatrick as one of his men, and Laura went along as horse tender. In the absence of the Sundance Kid, who was already in South America with Etta Place, Cassidy chose a newcomer, Deaf Charley Hanks, and the last man was Kid Curry. It was their plan to make the "big coup" and then all retire to Argentina to join Longabaugh, who was even then in the process of buying a ranch in the interior.

The man who replaced Longabaugh—Deaf Charley Hanks—was born Orlando Camilla Hanks in San Augustine, Texas, in 1876, son of Orlando Thacker "Bud" Hanks and Susan Pernella Thacker. Charley's great-aunt was none other than Nancy Hanks Lincoln, mother of President Abraham Lincoln. His grandfather, Horatio McMullin Hanks, had been a pioneer of Texas, having died in San Augustine in 1854, but his grandmother, Nancy Ann Thacker Hanks, survived until March 10, 1905.

When Orlando Camilla Hanks was approaching his early teens, his father died, leaving a family of seven boys and twin girls. His mother, Susan, then remarried, to James Cox, and the family moved to his ranch near Yorktown, DeWitt County, Texas.

James Cox killed the son of his neighbor, Homer Etsell, in a feud over cutting a wire fence, and Etsell thereby killed Cox. Deaf Charley, still in his teens, strapped on his gun and killed Etsell's fifteen-year-old son and then Etsell himself. A week later he encountered Etsell's teenage daughter on the road and pistol-whipped her and then raped her.

Deaf Charley escaped to Corpus Christi and then to Las Vegas, New Mexico, where he killed a man in the Buffalo Hall Saloon and then fled to Brown's Park in Utah.

At this time, Deaf Charley had not surpassed his sixteenth year, but his career flourished even more when he participated in several robberies with the Blackjack Ketchum gang, killed a lawman in New Mexico, killed two other men and raped two girls in Trinidad, Colorado, robbed a stagecoach near Denver, and fled to Montana.

On the night of August 25, 1893, Hanks and three companions robbed a train of the Northern Pacific near Greycliff, Montana, and escaped with $92,000. One month later the gang was captured on the Blackfoot Reservation and in the ensuing battle, three of the outlaws were killed, together with a lawman named Schubert.

Hanks, under the alias of Charles Jones, was sentenced to ten years in the Montana penitentiary at Deer Lodge on January 10, 1894, was released on April 30, 1901, and almost immediately was recruited to aid in the train robbery at Exeter.

Kid Curry chose the robbery site, and Cassidy went to St. Paul, Minnesota, where he learned of a shipment which could approach $100,000 going through on July 3. Cassidy arrived back in Montana about one week prior to the robbery.

On July 3, 1901, the Oriental Limited of the Great Northern Railroad stopped at Malta, Montana, seven miles from the proposed robbery, and Kid Curry climbed onto the baggage car behind the coal tender. Conductor Smith spotted him shortly after the train began to move and, believing him to be a tramp, ran to the side of the baggage car and ordered him off. The Kid pulled his six-shooter and told Smith, "Mind your own gawddamned business!" George Campbell, an acquaintance of Kid Curry, witnessed this event from the window of the local saloon.

Sheriff Griffith of Great Falls was on the train and conductor Smith informed him of the man on the blind baggage car and Griffith suggested that they stop at Exeter and put him off, and Smith then signaled engineer Thomas Jones.

When they approached Exeter, Thomas Jones began to slow the train to a halt, but Kid Curry came over the coal tender and into the cab and put his six-shooter in Jones' ribs and pulled another gun to cover fireman C. H. Smith and ordered the train pulled just short of a bridge. When the train came to a stop, brakeman Whiteside stepped down from the back car and started to run back toward Malta to spread the alarm but was stopped when Deaf Charley Hanks shot him in the arm and brought him back to the train.

As the train stopped near the bridge, Butch Cassidy, Ben Kilpatrick, and Laura Bullion came out from under it, all armed with Winchesters. Laura dropped to the offside of the train and kept the passengers' heads inside while Cassidy uncoupled the cars from the baggage and express sections with the aid of Kilpatrick.

Sheriff Griffith leaned out one of the windows and took several shots at Kid Curry, who returned the fire instantly, and Griffith ducked to the floor of the car and one of the shots wounded Mr. Douglas of Clancy, Montana, auditor of the Great Northern Railroad. Douglas was wounded in the shoulder and young Gertrude Smith of Tomah, Montana, was struck in the arm.

Cassidy and Kilpatrick now had the cars uncoupled and Cassidy rode the express car across the bridge while Kid Curry forced the engineer to move the engine. Curry then sent conductor Smith back through the cars to warn anyone against coming outside until they were gone.

Cassidy soon had the express car and safe blown with dynamite and by the time they had the money sacked, Deaf Charley and Laura Bullion were there with the horses and they rode off quickly toward the Mike O'Neill ranch.

At about two-thirty in the afternoon, George Cunningham, a local rancher, happened upon the scene and rode up toward the outlaws. Kid Curry motioned him back, but Cunningham continued, so Curry fired a shot close to Cunningham's horse. But when Cunningham still did not turn around, Curry put a shot through Cunningham's horse's neck, sending it stampeding into the hills with its rider.

The robbery netted the outlaws $65,000, $41,000 of which were in unsigned bank notes drawn on the National Bank of Montana at Helena. The first two posse members to set out on their trail were Byron Hurley and Tim Maloney of Malta, who headed out to cut them off, but halfway discovered that they had forgotten their guns.

Sheriff Griffith organized a posse of about forty men at Glascow, equipped with night wranglers, a chuck wagon, and other cumbersome gear that caused such slow travel that they made it only to Landusky the first night; there they started to get drunk and shoot up the town. Justice of the Peace Guy Manning issued arrests for the entire posse!

E. E. "Boo" MacGilvra of Butte, Montana, in a letter to Kerry Ross Boren, stated:

My father-in-law . . . Jake Myers, "Ol' Griz" . . . was the wagon boss for the Circle C outfit [Coburn ranch]. . . . Ol' Griz was at the Abe Gill ranch when the train was held up at Wagner [Exeter]—the posse trailing the Kid and his gang stayed overnight at the Gill ranch when trying to close in on the gang. Ol' Griz told me he counted eighty-six saddles in the yard that night.

The Kid and gang were on top of Thornhill Butte, camped there for a few days before scattering. From the top of the Butte they could see the country for miles and their camp fires were visible for miles. The posse knew the Kid was up there, but they never attempted to close in on him. Instead they had more or less of a picnic at the Gill place and in Landusky, not too far away, and disbanded without tangling with the outlaws.

Some of the outlaws dropped by the Mint Saloon at Great Falls and tried to induce the proprietor, Sid Willis, to pass some of the stolen money over his bar, but Willis declined. The outlaws then forged their own signatures to the notes, especially Ben Kilpatrick, whose handwriting in their estimation most closely resembled that of a banker.

Within a week of the robbery, Butch Cassidy appeared alone at Linwood, Utah, on the fringe of Brown's Park, where he had supper and slept one night in the back room of the Keith Smith home. Curry remained in Montana long enough to kill Jim Winters on the morning of July 26, 1901, aided by Kilpatrick and Hanks, and Laura was probably nearby with the horses when the Kid ambushed Winters as he stooped over a rain barrel to brush his teeth. The murder of Winters had been in retaliation for the killing of the Kid's brother, Johnnie Logan.

Kid Curry, Kilpatrick, Hanks, and Laura Bullion then rode south and appeared at Rawlins, Wyoming, where Curry buried a portion of his loot on Twenty-Mile Ranch, and then "hooked" a train and appeared next to Fanny Porter's place in Fort Worth, Texas.

On November 7, 1901, a jeweler in St. Louis, Missouri, deposited as part of his weekly earnings four notes drawn on the National Bank of Montana at his local bank, the Merchant's National Bank of St. Louis. A sharp-eyed clerk named Victor Jacquemin noticed something odd about the signatures and checked them against a stolen list and discovered that they were from a Montana train robbery, and he notified the Pinkertons.

The man who passed the forged note had given his name as John Arnold, but was in reality Ben Kilpatrick, and by mere chance on the following day, November 8, he was spotted passing in a buggy and was followed to Manley's Saloon and then to a boardinghouse at 2005 Chestnut Street. One of the Pinkertons staggered up the sidewalk as if drunk, bumped into the tall outlaw, and then wrestled him quickly to the ground, as other agents came to his aid. In "Arnold's" pocket they found a key to a room at the Laclede Hotel and there they found "Mrs. Rose Arnold" about to check out.

Neither Ben Kilpatrick nor Laura Bullion would break under questioning. On Ben they found a bank book inscribed "Harry Longabaugh, Fort Worth, Texas," and headlines broke that the infamous Sundance Kid had been captured in St. Louis, but after three days of grueling interrogation by Chief of Detectives Desmond, Kilpatrick finally admitted his real identity.

On December 12, 1901, Kilpatrick was sentenced to fifteen years in the federal penitentiary at Columbus, Ohio, for "forgery." On the following day Laura Bullion—still insisting that her real name was Della Rose, alias Laura Casey, alias Bullion—was sentenced to five years at the correctional institution at Jefferson City, Tennessee.

Meanwhile, the *St. Louis Globe-Democrat* stated that it had been reported that Butch Cassidy and the Sundance Kid had been in St. Louis, apparently planning to break Kilpatrick out of jail, but it had not been Cassidy and Sundance, but rather Cassidy and Kid Curry. Curry had taken Annie Rogers, his Texas girlfriend, and Deaf Charley Hanks as far as Mena, Arkansas, and Hanks had gone on to Memphis. Curry and Cassidy then met in St. Louis, but any plans to help Kilpatrick were thwarted when news of their presence hit the newspapers. Said Chief Desmond, "If they come, we are ready for them."

Meanwhile, Hanks had tried to pass some of the forged notes in the Nashville National Bank, was recognized, and after a gun battle with a bank guard, barely escaped out of town. He went to Calaveras County, California, briefly and then back to Texas, where he was finally tracked down and shot to death at San Antonio on April 16, 1902.

When Cassidy and Kid Curry attempted to smuggle a note to Kilpatrick at St. Louis through his lawyer, it was intercepted. Curry then caught a train west to retrieve some of his buried loot from the ranch near Rawlins and returned with enough to pay for Kilpatrick's expensive lawyers.

Curry then went to Asheville, North Carolina, where

he robbed a bank, and then appeared in Knoxville, Tennessee, under the alias of Will Wilson. On December 11, 1901, he shot two policemen, Dinwiddie and Saylor, who attempted to arrest him during a saloon brawl at the Ike Jones Saloon, and two days later was captured traveling disguised as a hobo in the woods near Jefferson City (where Laura Bullion had recently been transferred) and returned to Knoxville.

Logan insisted that his name was Charley Johnson and that he was from Chelsea, Iowa, but two thousand dollars in unsigned bank notes were found on his person and two claim checks led law officers to two bags at the railroad station containing a loaded single-action .45 with a ten-inch barrel and more unsigned currency wrapped in a *Cincinnati Times-Star* newspaper dated December 4.

In prison, Kilpatrick had obtained notes from Kid Curry through the grapevine and, through the same method, smuggled notes to Laura Bullion, several of which noted his concern at not having heard from Cassidy. He told Laura that the "kid" was becoming concerned over why "C" hadn't contacted him or made some effort to spring him from prison. Of course, neither of them knew at that time that Cassidy had already left for South America.

Laura Bullion was arrested with Ben Kilpatrick in St. Louis on November 8, 1901, and on December 13 was sentenced to the penitentiary in Jefferson City, Tennessee, for a term of five years. She was released in March 1906 and soon after took possession of a boardinghouse at 87 Central Avenue, Atlanta, Georgia, where Kilpatrick had been transferred. The boardinghouse was opposite the prison.

On June 27, 1903, Harvey Logan escaped the "impregnable" Knox County Jail in Tennessee just hours before he was to be transferred to the Columbus, Ohio, federal penitentiary. Before leaving Tennessee, Logan had somehow smuggled word to Ben Kilpatrick, who in turn smuggled a note out of prison to Laura Bullion which read: "The Kid is trying to locate C. [Cassidy] and get out of the country." Curry next appeared in the West masterminding another robbery to acquire funds to reach Cassidy in Argentina.

Logan first appeared at Hole-in-the-Wall in Wyoming and recruited Tom O'Day, but O'Day was captured soon after and Curry then went to Texas and acquired the aid of George Kilpatrick (the tall Texan's brother), and passing through Clinton, Texas, they recruited two other men, Bill Daly and Jim York.

On the evening of June 7, 1904, Logan and his companions held up the Colorado Midland train No. 5 near Parachute, Colorado, but in their haste, discovered that they had held up the wrong train and escaped with only a few thousand dollars in loose jewelry and some loose specie in a bag.

A posse soon pursued them, and in the ensuing battle at the foot of Mamm's Peak, Jim York was killed with Kid Curry's gun in his hand, and Curry and Kilpatrick escaped by leaping into the Grand River at Garfield Canyon in a daring plunge, Daly having left them a few days before. The body of Jim York, possessing Curry's gun (Colt .45, #147144), was erroneously identified as that of Kid Curry by the Pinkertons.

Less than one month following the Parachute robbery, Kid Curry and George Kilpatrick were seen in Brown's Park, Utah, and an informant notified Union Pacific detectives that the two outlaws were planning a train robbery in the same vicinity as the earlier Tipton job.

Union Pacific officials outfitted a special train equipped with the Super Posse, under the leadership of Nathaniel K. Boswell, and spread the rumor that the train carried a large amount of gold and currency. They made several runs between Cheyenne and Rock Springs, but while they rode the rails, Kid Curry and George Kilpatrick held up the bank at Cody, Wyoming.

The two outlaws were pursued by a posse led by none other than Buffalo Bill Cody, but the pursuit turned

into a hunting trip after the first day, and all thought of
the outlaws was abandoned. After a period of extended
travel through Texas and Mexico, Curry and Kilpatrick
made it to Argentina and joined Cassidy and Longabaugh.

Just when Laura Bullion arrived in South America is
uncertain, but she was certainly there in the company of
George Kilpatrick by the fall of 1907. Apparently Laura
wanted to purchase a ranch and a new life for herself
and for Ben Kilpatrick when he was released from
prison in 1911. She joined a gang which then consisted
of the Sundance Kid (alias Bob Evans, alias Bud
Evans), Harvey Logan (alias Andrew Duffy, alias
Hood), a young man believed to have been Lew Mc-
Carty (alias William, or Willie Wilson), Harry Nation,
Dick Clifford, Tom Dilly, Ansel Gibbons, George Kilpatrick, and others.

Deputy sheriff of the frontier police Alejandro Na-
varro, in a statement recorded in 1912, related that
". . . in 1908 Roberto Evans [Longabaugh] appeared
in Río Pico [Argentina] selling sheep to settlers of that
area."

In January 1908 a man riding over the Pampa de Cas-
tillo passed four horsemen with a string of fine thor-
oughbred horses. There were three *gringos* and a
Chilean peon. Closer examination revealed that one of
the *norteamericanos* was a woman dressed as a man. Although many have thought this to have been Etta Place,
it was instead Laura Bullion.

That evening the horsemen, minus the woman,
stopped at the hotel of Cruz Abeijón at La Mata, where
they introduced themselves as Bob Evans and Willie
Wilson, and said they were looking for land.

After having breakfast the *norteamericanos* inquired
of Abeijón the name of the best hotel in Comodoro
Rivadavia, and leaving the Chilean in charge of their
horses, they rode the three leagues into the town.

Comodoro Rivadavia was a small town nestled between the cliffs and the sea. The men stayed one week

and then returned to Abeijón's, bringing toffees for his children, and took their horses. When they left, Abeijón discovered that his telephone wire had been cut.

At one o'clock on the afternoon of February 3, 1908, Evans and Wilson attempted to rob the makeshift bank at Casa Lahusen in Comodoro Rivadavia, but Wilson got into an argument with the Chilean who held their horses and Evans had to break it up. Police Commissioner Barros heard the arguing and came running, just as Wilson shot the Chilean through the hand. Barros ran to his station and retrieved a sub-machine gun and fired at the outlaws as they rode out of town. Four mounted police pursued the outlaws but turned back after only a short way. That evening a Basque heard them singing to an accordion at their camp fire.

On June 11, 1911, Ben Kilpatrick was released from prison and he headed immediately for Texas. He then planned a robbery by which he might obtain funds for his proposed flight to South America, where he would join his beloved Laura, but it was not to be for either of them. On March 13, 1912, Ben Kilpatrick, alias the Tall Texan, was killed by messenger Trousdale while attempting to rob the Sunset Limited train near San Angelo. But it really didn't matter, because Laura had preceded him in death. Maybe he knew about it; maybe not.

Early in 1911, following the kidnapping and ransom of Ramos Luis Otero, a prominent Buenos Aires socialite, by Wilson and Evans [Longabaugh and McCarty], the minister of the interior ordered an all-out manhunt to clear the Cordillera of outlaws. A local newspaper, *La Prensa,* reported: "The Governor of Chubut informed the Minister of the Interior that he has taken severe measures to capture the bandits who are wandering through the territory. . . ."

In August 1911, shortly after the kidnapping of Otero, three *bandidos yanquis* rode into Mercedes with plans to rob the bank. The three outlaws were later found to be two men and a woman, the latter dressed in male attire. Pinkertons later identified the three as being Butch Cassidy, Harry Longabaugh, and Etta Place, based upon the following report filed by Pinkerton agent Frank Dimaio:

> In 1912, while General Superintendent of the Pittsburgh division, including Cleveland, Detroit, and Cincinnati offices, I visited Detroit and one evening went to an Italian restaurant there. Only one other person was in the restaurant at the time and when the lights were turned on this patron looked across at me and said: "Hello, Dimaio." I immediately recognized him as a Mr. Steele, a traveling salesman whom I had met in Buenos Aires. I invited him to my table. Mr. Steele said: "I have some very important news for you." Upon inquiring the nature of it, he said: "You recall the man Place, his wife and Parker whom you were looking for in the Argentine? Well, I was in Mercedes last year visiting my trade. When I returned to the hotel one of the guests said to me, 'Lift up the tarpaulin on the piazza.' Upon doing so I saw the bodies of Place, his wife and Ryan. They had been shot to death while holding up a bank in a nearby village."

The assumption has always been made that the town in question was Mercedes, Uruguay, but even Dimaio was uncertain of this. Recent evidence leads us to believe it was instead the town of Villa de Mercedes in Argentina. Pinkerton files contain the report of "agent No. 85," who reported under date of March 21, 1909:

> In regard to the Wild Bunch, will say that the last time I saw any of them was last June [1908]. Then I saw only Harry Longabaugh. I met him at Villa de Mercedes which is 475 miles west of Buenos Aires. . . . Harvey Logan is with him there. . . .

The identity of the three killed bank robbers are now known with reasonable certainty to have been Johnny Dey, Tom Dilly, and Laura Bullion.

George Kilpatrick had arrived in South America concurrent with Kid Curry following the Parachute, Colorado, train robbery and the robbery of the bank at Cody, Wyoming.

Tom Dilly, a former partner in the Patmos Head Land and Cattle Company near Sunnyside, Utah, had been a suspect in the killing of Sheriff Tyler and Deputy Jenkins in Utah (a crime perpetrated instead by Kid Curry) and in 1901 sold a herd of company cattle at Kansas City and absconded with the money to join others in South America.

In 1908 Laura Bullion was living with George Kilpatrick and Kid Curry on Curry's ranch near San Rafael, about one hundred and forty miles from Villa de Mercedes.

Laura Bullion was holding the horses for Johnny Dey and Tom Dilly when something went awry, and the three of them were shot down in the dusty streets of Villa de Mercedes. After photographs were taken, the bodies were covered with a tarpaulin.

News that the three had been killed reached the ears of friends in the United States, but they were identified as Cassidy, Longabaugh, and Etta Place. Matt Warner and Elza Lay were concerned over the identity, and with the aid of other friends, such as J. K. W. Bracken, paid the expenses of two men who knew Cassidy and Longabaugh intimately—Joe Walker, most notably—to go to South America and obtain copies of the photographs and establish the identities of the three outlaws.

Bracken's conclusion was that one of the men was without any question Tom Dilly, who had once been foreman for Bracken, but the identity of the other man and the woman, he knew not. Matt Warner related to his daughter, Joyce Warner, still residing in Price, Utah, that Cassidy was not among the photos and that the other man had not been Longabaugh and the woman was not Etta Place, but Laura Bullion.

Laura Bullion, alias Della Rose, alias Casey, reached her inevitable destiny. Fate does not always decree the final end, but the odds frequently do. However, the origin and final end of Laura Bullion is not quite so mysterious as it once was, and she takes her place in the dubious honor roll of the ladies of the Wild Bunch.

George Kilpatrick was killed in 1912 at Río Pico, Argentina.

2. ✓

Cattle Annie and Little Breeches— Oklahoma Delinquents

They were a pair of wild young girls in this even younger piece of the West called Oklahoma Territory. Annie McDougal—whom one writer calls McDouglet without giving any source—and Jennie Stevens, their proper names. But history would record them under nicknames as Cattle Annie and Little Breeches (or Britches).

How they acquired these apt monikers seems uncertain. Cattle Annie is said to have earned hers by serving as lookout for beef-rustling gangs before getting mixed up with the Doolin gang of bank and train robbers. Little Breeches may have gotten that road brand by donning male-style trousers befitting her small height.

The one known picture of these rough-and-ready young women shows Annie holding a shotgun, wearing the dragging long skirts of that period. Little Breeches is portrayed as what she was: a feisty little girl ready to side a bandit in a bout of love or robbing a train. The girls are said to have been seventeen and sixteen respectively when this picture was taken.

They were part of the homesteader inundation of western Indian Territory after that section had been detached to form Oklahoma Territory. The two girls resisted all efforts of parents to "raise them right" and were soon into all kinds of unladylike behavior, including horse stealing and prostitution. "Girl pards"—an equivalent of the modern girlfriends—they became in Western lingo. Their close pals and customers became the cowboys—those who had survived the nester annexation of so much rangeland and others finding it hard to adjust to these dadblamed new times.

At age fifteen, Jennie developed a false-pregnancy scare, so she married an upright young farmer who'd been mooning around her. After a few months of what was considerably less than married bliss, the young wanton drifted back into prostitution. Her outraged husband took her home to her father, then got a divorce.

So the girls chummed up increasingly with their friends the cowboys. Among them they heard much admiring comment about the original Dalton gang, composed of Oklahoma ex-cowhands of a hard stripe till its rout at Coffeyville, Kansas, on October 5, 1892. Plenty of Oklahomans remembered the Daltons; many admired them for preying off the banks and railroads. Their stature as lamented folk heroes mounted after the Coffeyville rub-out.

Bob and Grat Dalton were dead from the well-aimed bullets of Kansas citizens. Emmett, their younger brother, was in the second year of a long stretch at the Kansas state pen. Bill Dalton, maintaining till that time a respectable front, was now co-commander of a new gang succeeding the first—the Doolin-Dalton bunch—with his sometimes jealous comrade-at-arms, Bill Dalton, sharing leadership as well as loot.

Both Annie and Jennie sentimentalized about lanky Mr. Doolin, who was sometimes seen around this area of Oklahoma, particularly when on the dodge from Kansas posses. Wasn't he from Arkansas, like themselves? Didn't he, in the classic Robin Hood legend, steal from the rich and give to the poor?—or at least the poor cowboys said so. Wasn't Doolin, like the wide-eyed girls, lacking in formal education? Though Annie and Jennie could read and write tolerably well, the arts of literacy were still somewhat difficult for outlaw Bill.

The two kept hoping to meet the noted long rider. They did, and a new chapter of their lives began opening. During the spring or summer of 1894, the girls were squired to a country dance somewhere in Pawnee County. No invitations were issued to these affairs. Anybody who wanted to come, did. The guests that evening included not only the usual settlers and young people, but also some prominent members of the Doolin-Dalton gang.

Among those present were Little Dick West, Little Bill Raidler (said to have been a college graduate), Dynamite Dick Clifton, Bitter Creek Newcomb (alumnus of the original Dalton gang), and, some say, that battle-scarred Dalton brother, Bill.

The girls' heads swam when they were introduced to these luminaries of outlawry. They loved the distinction of being swung in waltzes and reels by the same hands that had robbed trains and gotten the drop on marshals.

Over in an appropriate corner madly fiddling sat the Great One himself—Bill Doolin, that bold buckie from back home in Arkansas. Annie, not knowing then that he was married, always felt that he cut down on a Texas-style fandango with even more spirit when he saw her smiling at him from the whirling crowd.

The sounds of the fiddle rose sensuously. A plunking banjo accompanied it. A nester from some creek bottom was puffing on a French harp, called in our time harmonica. Hands were clapping, feet pounding. Annie and Jennie had never known such a time.

They had met the elite of Oklahoma outlawry, had linked arms with them in the dance steps, been especially complimented by suave Bitter Creek, and been squired to the refreshment table by Charlie Pierce, who raced a fast horse for winnings when he wasn't out doing required chores of banditry for the two Bills.

The evening proceeded. More and more men were slipping out to jugs stashed in the bushes and downing raw red-eye. The longer a dance lasted, the larger the prospect of fights. This gathering was no exception.

Near midnight, two fellows who'd been eyeing each other tangled as a set was being danced. Friends of either took sides. Fists were flying when Bitter Creek Newcomb broke it up. He drew his .45 and shot out the lights.

Doolin danced with the girls during several sets. Names they mentioned were those of hard cases he knew. Besides, he may have heard from outlaw gossip of their involvement with horse and cattle thieves.

The two wild girls became the eyes and ears of the Doolin-Dalton gang after that evening of rustic revelry. This ensemble of trigger heisters needed such female aides to replace Robert Dalton's paramour, Flo Quick, dead from weapons fired by the citizens of Wichita, Kansas.

Up and down the lanes of northeastern Oklahoma rode the gang's new informants. The daring two picked up tips about the movements of sheriffs and marshals, passing them on to the quarreling cocaptains, Doolin and Dalton. They memorized networks of trails and roads. They learned to read signs and tracks like Indians. They became railroad buffs of a sort. Sometimes posing as a prospective passenger, one or the other girl would learn about the arrival and departure times of various trains. Through artless questions at depots they would find out which might be carrying shipments of bills and silver. They picked up timetables which reached the gang at its main base, Ingalls, the generally peaceful little town about forty miles south of Pawnee.

Until they became widely known, they came and went without interference at Guthrie, the territorial capital. They probably wore dresses on these trips to look like a pair of country girls come shopping for combs and ribbons. But from these jaunts they learned to recognize various marshals and deputy sheriffs pointed out to them by naïve townspeople.

They served as lookouts during various train and bank robberies attributed to the gang. These young ladies born to horsemanship could be safely entrusted with the getaway ponies and have them waiting for their owners once the swag had been collected.

In between larcenies the girls helped individual members steal steers and horses for contraband markets in

Kansas. They rode with various chums peddling whiskey to Indians in the Osage hills. Selling booze to tribesmen was legally forbidden throughout America, but the late Bob Dalton had been the leading bootlegger of those hills while serving by federal court appointment as police chief of the Osage Nation.

Cattle Annie and Little Breeches purportedly shed their last morals along with any residues of their religion after becoming what we would call today gun molls. But names of definite lovers are hard to come by and it is almost certain that each had more than one.

Historian Zoe (Mrs. Bill) Tilghman wrote in her excellent little work on Oklahoma baddies, *Outlaw Days,* that Cattle Annie fell deeply in love with a man when she was eighteen. But whether outlaw or honest settler, his name is not given.

A 1979 novel *Cattle Annie and Little Breeches* contains, among much other made-up fiction, the characterizations of Annie and Bitter Creek Newcomb being girlfriend and boyfriend. The author describes Newcomb as being "a half-breed Indian." But so far as is known, nobody of Indian descent ever rode with either of the gangs connected with the Daltons.

Newcomb probably had a lot of women, although he was no paragon of anything. His main light-o'-love was said to be Sadie Conley, his Ingalls mistress and widow of a marshal slain in a saloon brawl. But nothing has been found in his saga of tomcatting to connect him with either Cattle Annie or Little Breeches.

Similarly the author of that purplish novel concocts a romance between Little Breeches and Bill Dalton, soon to join Grat and Bob in whatever hereafter. Bill Dalton was no model of matrimonial fidelity as Bill Doolin is reputed to have been.

But he did have a wife and children who had followed him from California, where he'd had political ambitions, to Oklahoma, where he'd started living up to the bad Dalton name. The family would finally wind up living under an assumed identity near Ardmore, Oklahoma, not far from the Texas line. Nothing tangible connects him with that prodigal child Jennie Stevens, alias Little Breeches.

Usually the long riders scattered between "jobs," keeping in touch with fellow members of the gang and their girl pards through grapevine contacts. During these lulls, Annie and Breeches would sometimes visit their homefolks.

Their parents had long since stopped trying to exercise any discipline over these prodigal daughters. Nice boys didn't try to date them—at least not openly—for fear of losing out with nice girls. At that time, Breeches and Annie were generally rated by all nice people as being just ornery little whores instead of bandit aides. But their real calling was bound to come out in a territory whose main source of news was folk gossip.

Marshals and county sheriffs began noticing that a pair of hard-looking young girls were seen around various towns just before bank or railroad holdups. When lawmen compared descriptions, they all resembled those hussies in Pawnee County. Stoolies among nesters supplied the names of the girls and said that they had come visiting on behalf of "friends" believed to be the Doolin-Dalton buckies.

However, the young women could not be arrested on mere suspicion. U.S. Marshal Bill Tilghman ordered that they be kept under as much surveillance as possible in a land with so many hideouts. Officers questioned the frightened parents of each. Both girls were absent from home. The quavering families professed ignorance of where they might be. Nor could they be found in a search extending across eastern Oklahoma.

It is thought that they were waiting out the tempest by lying low. Some folklore says that they hid in a spacious cave on Turkey Creek near Ingalls. This cavern was so large that it could have easily contained the entire gang.

It is also supposed that they might be concealed in the notorious and well-named Robbers Cave in the Creek Nation of Indian Territory. But tribal police could not confirm their presence in this stretch, which is now the eastern half of Oklahoma state. Nor could federal marshals especially charged to track down white desperadoes holed up in Indian country.

Other reports said that the girls had fled to the red-light districts of various tough towns including Tulsa, Oklahoma; Wichita, Kansas; and Denison, Texas. Nothing came of these leads. Astute Marshal Tilghman believed that friends of the pair had circulated these rumors to confuse the law enforcers.

A new epidemic of bank robberies hit Oklahoma. The little girls from Pawnee played their part in spreading the infection.

They cased banks, noting where guards were usually stationed. Many country financial centers had none at all. They recalled locations of entrances and exits—particularly to see if the places had back doors through which robbers could escape easily after stealing the cash up front. They kept ears open to learn in what sections vigilante groups like the much-feared Anti-Horse Thief Association operated.

At home they kept trying to give the impression that they had reformed and settled down.

The community was unimpressed.

So far as the gang itself was concerned, the girls seem to have been forbidden territory. No plausible stories connect them with dalliance inside the group. Bill Doolin himself may have seen to that. For underneath his jovial manner, the outlaw chief kept a tight rein. Nothing more might disrupt his close club of men than feuding over a pair of loose women. That he would have well known.

Meantime, the nineteenth century was on its way out—the twentieth century on its way in. Frontier outlawry was fading along with the frontier.

Oklahoma Territory was becoming a country of new roads and of rail lines increasingly well guarded. New towns and counties were emerging from what had been mazes of sage and broomweed. Each of these units had more or less competent peace officers. All these cooperated with officials in Guthrie, the territorial capital, to realize one major objective: admission of the young territory as the newest state of the American Union.

However, Congress was holding back on enacting legislation because the long riders kept making so many headlines in the national press. Yet the outlaw is more often history's casualty than its interpreter. He reads no handwriting on walls, but simply makes adjustments which do not preserve him and his cohorts.

The campaign against outlawry stepped up in Oklahoma, eager for statehood. Law-and-order forces rallied around sharp-minded federal marshals like Chris Madsen, Steve Burke, and Heck Thomas. Thieves started going down before the bullets of posses. Bill Doolin had to divide his gang into small squadrons perpetrating this or that criminal act.

Bill Dalton had been the first headliner to go. He died under a marshal's bullet near Ardmore, Oklahoma, on June 8, 1894, following a bank robbery in Texas. Coffeyville had been no warning to him, but law-abiding citizens regarded his death as an omen of things to come.

Neither did those two wild girls draw any inferences from the fadeout of Mr. Dalton. They kept following blindly Bill Doolin, who didn't seem worried by this offensive of the badge wearers. They brought food, ammunition, and messages to whatever hiding place he directed. However, lawmen again noticed that this pair of tough-looking young women were seen often near places which had experienced a gang visitation or were about to do so.

Cattle Annie behaved haughtily toward a marshal she met on a trail. At this time the officer didn't know who she was, but he made a note of the occurrence.

Supposedly Little Breeches went back to her old trade of love for hire. The two started meeting more outlaws, less distinguished than the Doolin bunch, at more country dances. Then hard men on the prowl began stopping at Cattle Annie's home seeking hospitality. Her parents might not have liked the looks of these guests. But it was a tradition of the West to feed and bed every passing stranger without quizzing him about his personal life.

Meantime, Annie also pursued romantic interests not connected with her role as standby for the Doolin gang. At a dance she met a freebooter who captured her lonely heart. This person, name unrecorded, was anxious to find steady employment with Doolin. Annie, it is believed, volunteered to put in a word for him.

On a night that seemed promising, Annie donned male clothes stolen from a hired hand. Then the two lovebirds saddled up and headed toward the Rock Fort, a sort of outlaw roadside stop near Ingalls. Somewhere along the way her mount threw her right into the middle of an Oklahoma prairie, then it bolted off, leaving the hysterical swearing woman dependent for further transport on her boyfriend.

Instead, that ungrateful escort rode off, laughing loudly. His shocked sweetheart got up, dusted off the "borrowed" garments, then began trudging ten miles toward the house of people she knew.

She got them out of bed. A member of the family hitched up a buggy and drove the angry, upset lady home. Her own folks greeted her not with sympathy and commiseration, but with "jeers and taunts."

As if all this were not enough humiliation, the brutish lover appeared next day demanding the return of all the presents he had given her. Heartbroken, Annie turned them over. Then the tough girl cried like any female jiltee.

Civilization kept expanding in growing Oklahoma. Time kept shortening for the outlaws—major bandits like the Doolin ensemble and minor ones were being jailed or mowed down by marshals.

Time was also a waning something for outlaw sympathizers and informers. Through superb intelligence work, the marshals had gotten the name of two thousand—it is said—and with the aid of county sheriffs and grand juries were drilling them for evidence. Those who didn't cooperate with the law faced prosecution for aiding and abetting criminals.

Doolin tried to establish his own counterintelligence system of messengers recruited from discontented farmers and working in relay systems. Cattle Annie and Little Breeches were, of course, vital links in this setup.

Once the girls—by delivering messages passed on to still other couriers—kept the whole Doolin gang from being captured at the Rock Fort. Excited possemen, ready for an all-out battle, arrived at the place minutes after the bad actors had fled. More interference followed. Cattle Annie and Little Breeches were assigned by Doolin to watch roads for officers and posses. Also, they started stealing horses for their pards of the gang.

Chief Marshal E. D. Nix had endured a bellyful of their interference. He ordered arrests on specific charges of horse thievery. Cattle Annie was also suspected of a federal offense: selling whiskey to Indians. Whatever their misbehavior, Nix was determined to retire these two young criminals from circulation.

He sent two of his best men after them—Marshals Bill Tilghman and Steve Burke. Tilghman (pronounced Tillman) had been a Kansas deputy during the roaring years of the great cattle drives. Burke would go on to become a celebrated Baptist preacher. Carrying warrants, the lawmen trailed the girls to a farmhouse outside Pawnee. Little Breeches spotted them from a rear window as they reached the gate.

Quick as a wildcat, she leaped out the window onto the back of her horse. Then she was "cutting wind" across the prairie. "I'll get this one," Tilghman yelled to Burke. "You get the other." Tilghman spurred his horse in the direction of the fleeing woman.

Little Breeches turned in her saddle and drew a six-shooter. Bullets spewed past the marshal's ears and cheeks, barely missing his skull. At that moment Tilghman, an even better marksman, could have tumbled the then seventeen-year-old girl from her saddle. But in his long years of gunning, he was yet to kill a woman. Ducking to escape this woman's barrage, he unstrapped his Winchester rifle from the saddle side. Then he fired at the horse.

It dropped dead. Its owner tried to leap from the saddle as it went down, but her right leg was pinned under the animal. Tilghman dismounted. Six inches away from the girl lay her six-shooter, mockingly near but just out of her frantic grasp.

When her captor reached her, he said, "You are under arrest, miss. I'll take your gun." Her reply was a blast of obscenity. He unloaded the weapon, then lifted the dead horse from her.

Little Breeches was still unwilling to surrender. Her fists doubled. She landed a right on the marshal's jaw, then her long, sharp fingernails tore into his face. Tilghman swung her around. His heavy hand descended on the bottom of her dungarees, which took the fight out of the stubborn juvenile delinquent. Obediently she mounted Tilghman's horse, sitting behind him, grasping his belt.

When the two reached the farmhouse, they saw Marshal Burke in the front yard with Cattle Annie. He was clutching the screaming, kicking girl in a tight hold. His hat was gone, as well as some of his hair. His face was scratched and bleeding from her needle-sharp fingernails.

Like her companion, Annie had been sitting at a window when Burke had grabbed her from the ground. Surprised and cursing a blue streak, she had fallen atop the marshal. He won the wrestling match that followed, but at the cost of skin and hair.

Both girl pards were now retired from outlawry—Breeches at seventeen; Annie at eighteen. Their capture was a major blow to the increasingly shaky Doolin gang. Just about a year and a half afterward, Bill Doolin himself would be shot down in an ambuscade staged by Marshal Heck Thomas. With him at the time would be his respectable wife and infant son, with the three having been bound for New Mexico and a presumable fresh start.

Looking subdued but soiled, the girl prisoners were taken to Noble County jail at Perry, Oklahoma. There a matron removed the men's clothes they had been wearing and found dresses for them to wear instead. She also scrubbed and brushed them till they looked like what they were essentially—a pair of good-looking kids whose lives might still be changed.

The girls were brought up on multiple charges before Territorial Judge Brier, who had no mind to throw law books at defendants so young. Particularly not after Marshals Tilghman and Burke appeared before the court to ask leniency for them. The pair were given short sentences. They were ordered to do their time at a reformatory in Framingham, Massachusetts, since Oklahoma had no prison for female convicts.

From Oklahoma's problem teenagers they came its national celebrities. They traveled by interconnecting trains and in minimal custody. The thoughtful jail matron had seen that they were properly dressed and primped for this biggest event of their young lives. The American press gave them sensational coverage as the wild territory's young outlaws traveling to pay their debt to society. Not since the late Belle Starr had any Oklahoma woman been given so much lavish publicity.

Crowds lined railroad stops, hoping to get glimpses of the two. The girls waved and blew kisses at their cheering public. Here they were—alive and acclaimed—where Madame Starr had wound up shot to death on an Indian Territory back road.

There was a two-hour layover in Boston before the last lap to Framingham, so under surveillance, the young convicts were permitted to see a bit of that Yankee metropolis—so much bigger than Guthrie.

Cattle Annie took the big town in stride. Little Breeches squealed in delight. She noticed particularly the garb and gait of handsomely dressed women going in and out of resplendent shops. She sniffed avidly the restaurants, and she made up her mind that she would be returning to this magnificent city.

After two years the girls were released from the reformatory. From what can be inferred, the ex-lady outlaws had behaved correctly. Otherwise, they might have been detained longer. At any rate, we have no record of either girl being implicated in any further crimes, though for a time it seems that Little Breeches may have become a vagrant on the streets of New York.

Little Jennie Stevens had soon found her Boston idyllic picture dissolving in pans of suds and dishwater. The naïve country girl had found domestic employment: cooking, sweeping, doing laundry, and the like. But doing housework in this caste-bound city was very different from the same type of labor back home.

There "hired girls" and "hired men" mingled with their employer's families and took their meals at the same table. The word "servant" was not one of common usage in Oklahoma. But here in the homes of the well-off people, servants ate at separate tables, spoke usually only when spoken to, and had to show appreciation for enjoying such a status.

Yet somehow, this complex East had gotten into her blood and she didn't want to go back to simplistic Oklahoma. So, she moved on to an even larger eastern city two hundred miles away—New York.

She might have found low-paid employment in that largest of America's asphalt jungles. She might have walked the streets plying her old trade during jobless intervals. At some point she seems to have been rescued by a major charitable group, the City Missionary Society, and put to "settlement house" work, which could have meant anything from scrubbing banisters to waxing church furniture. She probably lived for a time in one of the society's neighborhood settlement houses.

Whether she remained a ward of the organization for that last portion of her waning life seems uncertain. The still existing City Missionary Society failed to answer an inquiry made in 1980 by Oklahoma-based writer Harold Preece. We do know that she contracted tuberculosis after two years in New York and that the disease may have been partially brought on by malnutrition. She died, still under twenty-five, about 1900 in New York's free institution, Bellevue Hospital. Some writers think that she was penniless at the time of her death.

Cattle Annie had by that time married a supposedly respectable man in Oklahoma, and later, it is said, moved with him to California. It is believed that the couple may have named their first child Jennie, after the blazing girl pard who had wound up as a pitiful waif back East.

During 1907, Congress had finally admitted to the Union the state of Oklahoma, created from a merger of Oklahoma and Indian territories. By now most of the old-time outlaws had either straightened up or been gunned down like jackrabbits by sheriffs and outlaws. The Dalton legend and Cattle Annie/Little Breeches story persisted as verbal relics of the past.

Then, in 1929, a spectacular ex-carnie calling himself Jack Dalton and claiming to be a nephew of *the* Daltons turned up. High over the city of Albuquerque, New Mexico, he married in a plane a publicity-loving lady styling herself "Cattle Annie" Burke.

This Dalton, from the wrong family, claimed to be a nephew of the illustrious bandits with whom he shared a surname. This claim was indignantly denied by Emmett Dalton, then a realtor in Los Angeles. Emmett said that the drifting old scoundrel was in no way related to the now very respectable Daltons of California and Missouri.

The new Mrs. Jack Dalton claimed to have been raised in Dewey County, Oklahoma, and slipped food to the bandit Daltons in the Glass Mountains near Taloga. Whatever her story, nothing indicates that the authentic Cattle Annie grew up in Dower County a long way from Pawnee County.

In 1949, Jack Dalton would resurface as J. Frank Dalton, claiming this time to be an alias of long-dead Jesse James, whom he pretended to be. Jesse, by his story, had not actually been shot by Robert Ford at St. Joseph, Missouri, in 1882. By this preposterous yarn, which St. Louis author Carl Breihan vigorously exposed, Jesse had gone underground after a purported gang member, Charlie Bigelow, had been shot down by his comrades, with his corpse later palmed off as that of America's foremost desperado.

"Cattle Annie" Burke Dalton didn't show up at this "encore." Harold Preece, leading authority on the Dalton gang, thinks that she had the same sort of vivid imagination as her husband. He believes that she stole the historic nickname of Cattle Annie from having operated a cattle ranch at Kingman, Arizona.

Unfortunately, much material on the real Cattle Annie and Little Breeches is believed to have been burned about 1971 in a mass destruction of smoldering records at the courthouse where they were tried.

To the sorrow of historians, old archives sometimes become extinguished like old memories—and with the same irreparable results.

3.

Rose Dunn: Rose of the Cimarron

No one was ever able to figure out just why the little town of Ingalls, Oklahoma, was ever brought into being. Situated in or near the Creek Nation, near the ranch of Bee Dunn, it was a meeting place of outlaws from the Indian Territory and elsewhere. It was nestled in a secluded spot between the Creek Nation and Stillwater, in a area which was broken, hilly, and covered by a dense growth of forest and underbrush. However, the immediate area around the town was fairly level and open country. Old Man Dunn, it is said, even built a kind of fort on his ranch, where outlaws on the run could hibernate while the law went looking for them. For a certain sum of money the Dunns, a large family, would see to it that the fugitives were not molested.

The town itself consisted mainly of one street, named Ash, sometimes even called Main Street. On the west side of this street were a half-dozen business houses, and on the south corner stood the Delph Livery Stable, flanked by Trilby's Saloon, Pierce's Livery Stable, Sander's Barber Shop, Brigg's Drug Store, and a general mercantile store operated by a man named Barry.

There were other business houses on the other side of the street as well—namely, Wagner's Blacksmith Shop, Murray & Ransom's Saloon, and Ketchum's Boot Store.

Behind this row of buildings stood the O.K. City Hotel, operated by Mary Pierce.

Murray & Ransom's Saloon and gambling house was, of course, the favorite spot in Ingalls; next in line was the Pierce place of ill-repute. Mrs. Mary Pierce was a good friend of the outlaws, so long as they shelled out heavily for her rooms and her girls.

It was in the area of Ingalls that Bill Doolin discovered a cave, which he stocked with supplies, thus creating another link in his escape route, should this become necessary. Another Bill visited Ingalls frequently, too. He was Bill Dalton, brother of the infamous Dalton band of robbers and killers.

It was now 1893 . . . the Daltons had been wiped out during the gang's abortive raid upon Coffeyville, Kansas, in the act of trying to rob two banks at the same time. Only Emmett Dalton remained alive after that fiasco—Bill had not been there—and now Emmett was serving time in the Lansing, Kansas, prison. A new brand of brazen outlaws sprang up soon after, known as the Dalton-Doolin band. This combine robbed a train at Wharton, Oklahoma Territory. At Spearville and Cimarron, Kansas, the same bunch robbed two more trains.

Finally word was sent the law officers that the gang was holing up at Ingalls several nights a week or more. A posse was at once organized, to be led by the veteran Bill Tilghman. However, Bill had broken an ankle and was confined to his home at Guthrie. It was now a deadly game of hide and seek as the redoubtable Bill Tilghman, Heck Thomas, and other noted officers took after the outlaws as they flitted from one train or bank to another. Bill Doolin was clever. He managed to throw off pursuit so effectively that the officers knew nothing of the band's whereabouts until they were informed of the Ingalls meeting place.

When in full swing, the Doolin-Dalton band consisted of Bill Doolin, Bill Dalton, Bitter Creek Newcomb, Charley Pierce, Roy Daugherty (alias Arkansas Tom Jones), Bill Raidler, Little Dick West, Oliver Yountis (alias Crescent Sam), Tulsa Jack Blake, Dynamite Dick

Clifton, and George Red Buck Waightman, the meanest of the lot.

The fight at Ingalls, which occurred on September 1, 1893, was the beginning of the end. The Ingalls fight indeed is one of the red periods in outlaw history.

The fight involved only Doolin, Dalton, Newcomb, Dynamite Dick, Tulsa Jack, Red Buck, and Roy Daugherty, who, although not actually involved in the shooting, was ill upstairs in the Pierce hotel. Sheriff John Hixon and his son, together with U.S. deputy marshals A. H. Houston, Lafe Shadley, Dick Speed, and Jim Masterson, formed the nucleus of the posse, other deputies arriving later.

The officers and possemen had disguised themselves as hunters, exploring in the area of Ingalls. Several days passed, with the scouts reporting that the gang had ridden into the town during the afternoon and had stabled their horses, some of the men going to Murray & Ransom's Saloon and others going to the Pierce hotel. Sheriff Hixon at once dispatched a message to John Hale and W. M. Nix, who were some fifteen miles west, requesting they join him as quickly as possible.

Hixon did not expect to launch a siege until the arrival of more deputies; his only thought now was to deploy his men in order that the escape of the outlaws would be prevented.

It was high noon when the two covered wagons carrying the lawmen drew close to Ingalls. Hixon ordered the teams stopped in a protecting ravine nearby and had his men ready for action. Each lawman was well equipped with several Colt revolvers and a Winchester rifle, with plenty of ammunition for both weapons.

After Deputy Dick Speed had unloaded his wagon, he drove it south on Ash Street, Ingalls' main street. He brought his team to a halt in front of Pierce's Livery Stable, alighted, and walked through the doorway, rifle in hand. He warned the owner not to try any funny business in trying to warn the outlaws that officers were nearby.

Bitter Creek Newcomb, unaware of what was going

on, stepped from the saloon and walked over to the livery stable, the one next to the saloon. It was later learned that he had intended to visit his girlfriend, Sadie Conley, whose residence was next to the O.K. City Hotel.

As Bitter Creek's horse tromped slowly down Ash Street, Deputy Speed thought that his position had been revealed in some manner. He stepped from the stable, rested his Winchester on a wagon wheel, and fired. His first shot struck Newcomb's rifle and smashed the magazine mechanism. The bullet also struck Bitter Creek in the groin, inflicting a serious wound. His rifle useless, Bitter Creek drew his revolver and shot Speed in the chest, killing him almost instantly. Newcomb, reeling in the saddle, then raced for the open door of the nearby Livery Stable. He dashed through the back door of the barn and raced toward the safety of a nearby draw. The fight at Ingalls was on!

When Newcomb had left the saloon, five of his friends remained there, playing poker. Arkansas Tom Jones had gone to the O.K. City Hotel to rest, due to an illness he was suffering. Doolin, Dalton, and Dynamite Dick had been joined by Tulsa Jack Blake and Red Buck Waightman shortly after the first group of outlaws had entered Ingalls and had gone to Murray & Ransom's saloon.

The five outlaws at the poker table leaped to their feet when the shootout between Speed and Newcomb occurred. They grabbed their rifles and made a dash for the livery stable. This daring and unexpected move caused the officers to change their positions. There was nothing they could do now but try to capture or kill the outlaws. Jim Masterson leaped behind a tree for protection from the whizzing bullets; Hixon had leaped into a shallow dip; Shadley and Houston were in the thick of things.

Some reports have stated that Bitter Creek Newcomb was wounded in the saloon and had been assisted to safety by Bill Doolin, with the aid of Dynamite Dick and Red Buck, but as has been stated, Newcomb was long gone.

Deputy Houston tried to run for the shelter of a tree and was killed by a shot from the hotel window. It has never been really known if Arkansas Tom was shooting from that vantage point or if the women were. Lafe Shadley dived behind the body of a dead horse for protection. From that point he poured a withering fire into the livery stable.

Again Newcomb comes into the picture: a story holds that Rose of the Cimarron, really Rose Dunn and reputedly the sweetheart of Bitter Creek, had been watching from an upstairs window of the hotel, had seen Newcomb drop, and had gone to his rescue. Legend has it that she buckled on two belts of cartridges about her waist, grabbed a Winchester, and dashed to the aid of her lover. She had accomplished this by using a rope to drop to the ground on the sheltered side of the hotel. Marshal Nix later said they were reluctant to shoot a woman and held their fire. It was even stated by some writers that Rose rode off with the outlaws and that it had been Doolin who had killed Dick Speed.

As the outlaws rode to the same draw Newcomb had used, Deputy Marshal Lafe Shadley saw them and raised his rifle, but before he was able to fire, he was wounded. He ran to the home of George Ransom but was refused admittance, being informed that the family was hiding in a nearby cave. Shadley was able to gain the safety of the cave but decided to get in another shot or two at the fleeing outlaws. However, as he appeared at the corner of the house, he was spotted by Bill Dalton, who fired several shots at him with his rifle. The officer was wounded and died several days later.

The escaping outlaws had forgotten about Arkansas Tom, who was still upstairs in the bullet-ridden O.K. City Hotel. He soon surrendered, a poor reward in exchange for the lives of three brave officers.

Arkansas Tom was arrested, taken to the jail in Payne County, although he swore he had not fired a shot during the entire fight, was later sentenced to serve fifty years in the territorial prison at Lansing, Kansas, on a charge of manslaughter. On May 21, 1894, he was taken to the prison and in 1908 was transferred to the Oklahoma State Penitentiary at McAlester. He was paroled on November 26, 1910, through the efforts of his brothers. He seemed to have reformed, but in 1917 he was involved in the holdup of the Neosho, Missouri, bank, captured, and sent to the Missouri State Prison at Jefferson City, to serve an eight-year term. He was discharged on November 11, 1921. Not long afterward he was accused of complicity in the Ashbury, Missouri, bank holdup and became a fugitive. On August 6, 1924, he was killed when he resisted arrest at Joplin, Missouri.

The Ingalls battle, told over and over again, each time being changed somewhat, created quite a sensation because of the story of Rose of the Cimarron. Who was this fabulous girl whose name had been kept a secret for years and whose story about her racing to the aid of Bitter Creek Newcomb has grown completely out of focus? The story of Rose, as told to me by her husband, in part by Rose herself, and by the son of Bill Doolin, bears out the probable fact that Rose was nowhere near Ingalls on that fateful day. Arkansas Tom, in an eyewitness account of the fight, and stories in contemporary newspaper items make no mention of Marshal Nix's story of the Rose of the Cimarron.

Some accounts have even claimed that Rose was later arrested and sent to the women's prison at Framingham, Massachusetts, for her part in the Ingalls matter. However, the records of the Department of Correction, Massachusetts Correctional Institution, fail to indicate the admission of any Rose Dunn during the time period involved. In fact, no record has been found of Rose ever being arrested for anything.

Yes, Rose's name was Dunn, and she was born on September 5, 1878. She earned the title of Rose of the Cimarron not because she rode with noted outlaws or because of the Ingalls fight and legend, but simply because she was a superb horsewoman and a good friend of the people living along the banks of the Cimarron. Her family was the noted Dunn ranching people of

Oklahoma, although most people said they aided the outlaws, for a price.

Rose married Charles Noble on December 5, 1897. Her first husband died in the early 1930s. The second man Rose married was Richard Fleming of Centralia, Washington. Mr. Fleming told me shortly before Rose's death: "These stories of Rose are untrue. It caused my wife a great deal of embarrassment all her life and forced her into virtual seclusion. She was a true friend of the outlaws and never betrayed them. But she never was the sweetheart of any one of them."

Fleming further stated that Rose was a little over sixteen when he met her in 1895 at a square dance at Ingalls, then a bustling trail town ten miles east of Stillwater. Had she ridden with outlaws and fought the marshals to save a sweetheart, as alleged, she hardly would have been in her teens at the time, he pointed out.

"Historical writers, digging into the rich lore of early Oklahoma, have argued Rose's place in history for over half a century. Some hold the Rose of the Cimarron tales to be true, others say they are false, and some declare there never was such a person," Fleming further pointed out.

Fleming also pointed out that contemporary newspaper accounts of the Ingalls fight failed to mention that a woman was involved, one way or another. He said that the story probably was hatched up in the imaginative brains of Bill Tilghman or E. D. Nix.

Fleming stated that he met Rose while visiting a brother who had homesteaded in Payne County at the opening of the Indian Territory. He was then seventeen. Fleming farmed in the area awhile, leaving in 1906 to study for the Roman Catholic priesthood.

"I had first heard her referred to as Rose of the Cimarron in 1895, soon after I came down there," Fleming told this author. "They called her that, but not because she was a bandit queen. She was a superb horsewoman."

Fleming moved to the West Coast and did not hear of Rose again until nearly forty years later. Both had married in the meantime; Fleming became a widower, and

Rose a widow. She lived in New Mexico for a number of years.

"About ten years ago, I was down in these parts again and asked about Rose. A friend took me to see her, and we got acquainted all over again."

They were married June 18, 1946, and lived in Washington until her death. Mr. Fleming now has also passed away.

This author will always remember Mr. Fleming's final words to him as he left their modest home in Centralia. "Rose was modest and detested notoriety. The legends woven about her name, the tales about her youth are lies. She shunned the publicity and remained in seclusion for many years."

Rose died in July 1955, still somewhat of a mystery to those who love Western lore.

It must be mentioned that there were several young women who acted as spies for Doolin. Bill Tilghman had learned that Cattle Annie and "Little Breeches" were petty thieves as well as Doolin spies. With Steve Burke, another deputy, he found the trail of the two girls and followed it to a farmhouse near Pawnee. Little Breeches dashed from the back door, mounted her horse, and galloped away. Tilghman followed her, while Burke dismounted and eased his way up to the house.

Tilghman's horse was faster, so he overtook the farm animal Little Breeches was riding. She turned in the saddle and fired several rifle shots at her pursuer, but all went wild. Too much the gentleman to fire at a woman, Bill shot and killed the girl's mount. The fallen animal pinned her leg and she was unable to escape. She struggled frantically to release her pistol, but was unable to do so. When Tilghman approached her, she cursed him and threw a handful of dust into his eyes. When he was able to control her, he placed her on his horse, got up behind her, and hurried back to the farmhouse, anxious to see how his partner had fared.

Burke had walked up to a window, looked in, and seen Cattle Annie peering in the opposite direction. She had a Winchester rifle in her hand. Just as she saw

Burke and was getting ready to fire, he grabbed her by the shoulders and yanked her through the window. He held her in a strong bear hug, which prevented her from drawing one of her revolvers.

Taken to Perry, Oklahoma, the girls were tried before Judge Brier and sentenced to the federal reformatory at Framingham, Massachusetts. They gave their names as Anile McDougal, alias Cattle Annie, and Jennie Metcalf (or Stevens), alias Little Breeches. They were daughters of the two poor families living in the Osage Nation. After their release from the reformatory, both girls lived in the New York slums.

As for Bill Dalton and Bill Doolin, this is what happened to them.

On September 25, 1895, the officers trailed Bill's wife to his home on the ranch of Houston Wallace. Bill and his two young children and a farmhand remained there while Mrs. Wallace and Bill's wife drove off to do some shopping. At noon Bill started for the barn to help the farmhand hitch up a team, and tarried long enough to play with his youngest child, Grace, who was a cripple. Suddenly the echo of gunfire rent the air and Bill Dalton fell dead to the ground. Bill's remains were buried on the property of his father-in-law at Livingston. Later it was reinterred in the cemetery at Atwater, California.

Bill Doolin met his end the night of August 25, 1896, at the Ellsworth home near Lawson, Oklahoma. At sundown that day Bill saddled his horse. He intended to check the trail before his family followed in a covered wagon. As he rode slowly down the trail, his .40-.82 Winchester ready for use, Heck Thomas and his posse in ambush went into action. Doolin was killed by a charge from a shotgun fired by Bee Dunn.

The body of Doolin was taken to Guthrie, where it was placed on exhibit at the Rhodes Undertaking Parlor. Later it was buried in the Summit View Cemetery, the grave marked only by a twisted buggy axle. Today a proper gravestone marks the last resting place of one of Oklahoma's greatest robbers.

As for Bitter Creek Newcomb, he managed to escape to a small cabin south of Ingalls. Dr. Bland of Cushing, Oklahoma, was summoned by Bill Doolin to attend Newcomb's wound. Although the wound was very serious and Bitter Creek had lost a lot of blood, he managed to survive until May 1, 1895, when he and Charlie Pierce were killed by Bee and John Dunn for the reward money.

4.

◆◆◆

Pearl Hart:
Lady Outlaw

Only the oldest residents of Arizona remembered the hell-roaring days of Tombstone and other towns of the desert wastelands near the turn of the century. People talked about the exploits of Wyatt Earp, Doc Holliday, Curly Bill, Johnny Ringo, and others, of course; but now, well, Arizona was as safe as Missouri or even Kansas, so far as the traveler was concerned.

Yes, things had changed. No longer were the fierce range wars in progress or the romanticized rustling and gunfights going on. The ranch country was a maze of fences and anyone caught placing his brand on another's cows was promptly and legally dealt with. Not by the use of the hanging tree, but by the actions of the courts, which held sway now, and everything was legal. Such a rustler would be prosecuted as vigorously as would be a burglar or a purse snatcher of some large Arizona city.

True, open gambling still existed, but not the hands-up collection system used so aptly by Jesse James and others of like ilk. The larger cities were even being subjected to a total changeover from the wild and woolly past to a scene of Sunday-school peace and quiet. A reformation move was sweeping the state, which once boasted some of the greatest outlaws and lawmen, to say nothing of the hellish feuds which were carried on not too many years before.

So when the set pattern of a new civilization was one day shattered to bits by a flare of the Old West in 1899, it brought comments from some of the oldsters, one of whom said, "By golly, just like the old times, sounds mighty good to me." Not that these old gentlemen were in favor of violence and robbery. They possibly felt like new again, like they had a place in the world, like the days back in the mining camps when they were somebody. It is difficult to transplant an old tree from the loam to the sand and not expect some drastic changes.

The news which echoed across the state was doubly unbelievable, for the incident was activated by a young girl not too many years out of a famous Canadian boarding school. In 1888 Pearl Taylor, age sixteen, came to the girls' school at Lindsay, Ontario, Canada. Slight and somewhat homely, Pearl nevertheless was soon carrying on an affair with Mr. Hart, a no-good young man who hung around town. To make matters worse, Pearl ran off with Hart in the early part of 1889.

Hart maintained no kind of permanent work, but applied what little talents he had to the dubious art of gambling and trying to earn money at the racetracks. Even though life was meager for Pearl at this time, she remained with Hart. In 1893 they went to Chicago, Illinois, where Hart worked at the World's Columbian Exposition. However, Hart's plans fell short of what he had anticipated. Instead of becoming associated with the professional gamblers of the fair, he was forced to act as a ticket-taker and semi-barker at one of the midway shows. The ignominy of it all was too much for Pearl Hart. She decided to return to her mother at Lindsay, Ontario.

There was nothing in her home town to excite the interest of Pearl Hart. She longed for the bright lights of Chicago, for the smell and noise of the rowdy crowds and the constant ring of the silver and gold at the gambling tables. The thrill of the Western rodeos and trick-shooting artists of the fair still haunted her. She wondered if the shoot-outs and the dusty streets still existed in the West, or if the false-front buildings still comprised most of the towns' buildings. Finally she decided she must see for herself.

It was not long before Pearl bought herself a one-way ticket to Trinidad, Colorado, with money provided by an admirer of the town. Her dreams of the West were quickly shattered, however, when she found that her "Buffalo Bill West" was simply an illusion, something that would burst with the simple prick of a pin. Pearl also quickly found that Trinidad was overrun with men of shabby character, but who had money and were willing to spend it on a girl if she treated them right.

"I'd marry you if you didn't already have a man," one of the cowboys told her. "As it is, we figure a girl without money or a family comes West to make a living, one way or other, and we know only one way."

Pearl Hart had little choice, actually. She was in a world entirely foreign to her, friendless and penniless, and really not caring too much what happened to her. Under these circumstances she plunged into a mode of life which was considered quite disreputable by the better element of the town, to say the least.

She became an expert at her trade and in two years was master of it. Pearl drifted around the western towns, selling her wares and learning to drink hard liquor with the best of them. Yet, when the occasion demanded, she could refuse a drink and remain perfectly calm under the pressure at hand. Now, her life was not exactly dull either. She had made friends with some of the old-timers, veteran gamblers, gunmen, and some ex-outlaws who were still about. From them she learned true stories of the excitement she had hoped to see in the West.

One day she ran into Calamity Jane, almost too full of beer to give an accurate account of what she was trying to tell. The meeting cast such a spell upon Pearl that she visited the noted frontierswoman in her room the next day to learn more about her association with Wild Bill Hickok.

"Were you and Hickok married?" Pearl wanted to know.

Quite sober now, Calamity Jane looked up. A sudden calmness seemed to pass over her face and a seldom-seen smile quivered at the corners of her mouth.

"Well, in a way, Pearl. We were married, but it never amounted to much. Bill was too ashamed of me and my wild ways for his fancy eastern friends. He left me before too long and I never bothered much about it. Maybe that's why I took to drinking beer the way I do."

Pearl felt sorry for Jane. She realized now that her own life was running a similar pattern, although she was not married to a man whose name carried the notoriety as did Bill Hickok's.

Calamity told Pearl that the sorriest day of her life was August 2, 1876, when Hickok was shot in the back of the head by Jack McCall in Deadwood, South Dakota. Pearl was fascinated by Calamity Jane's story of how she sat in on the trial of McCall and wanted to kill him when the miners' jury acquitted him. She told Pearl that she planned to follow McCall anywhere he went, to avenge the assassination of Bill Hickok.

"I always had a soft spot for Bill, regardless of how he treated me, and I was real happy when I found out that McCall was finally hanged for his crime," Jane told Pearl as they parted company. It was the last Pearl saw of Calamity Jane, the much-overrated gunwoman and Indian fighter of the West. Pearl felt real bad when she heard of Jane's death in 1903.

One day in Cheyenne, Pearl ran across Mrs. Agnes Lake Thatcher, the woman who married Wild Bill Hickok in March 1876. From her she learned that the famous gunman was once totally blind from a disease he had contracted, and how he had saved her from a horrible death of being clawed by lions. She had been a member of the famous Lake Troupe, known in circus annals from coast to coast. Agnes Lake had been in the lion tamer's ring when one of the animals went mad. Hickok rescued her by killing the lion with a revolver shot through the brain.

Pearl enjoyed the conversation and no doubt she is the only person to whom Mrs. Hickok spoke about this. At least, there seems no other record of such meetings between Mrs. Hickok and other persons.

In 1895 Pearl Hart was back in Phoenix, Arizona, where she ran into her husband on the street. He was taken back a little, but realized that she probably had made a little money, and now he wanted to get his share of it. In a way, Pearl was glad to see Hart, for she was tired of leading a dissipated life and of mingling with the rough elements of the saloons and dance halls of the city. She seemed ready to settle down.

So Pearl took the duties of a normal housewife. In two years she was the mother of two fine children. This turn of events frightened Hart; he was no family man and wanted to be on the loose again. Pearl sent the children to her mother and left Hart again. She did not return to her previous mode of living, however, but visited the various mining camps and worked as a servant girl. She also applied this talent to some of the better homes in the large cities. It all worked out well until Hart followed her again and tried to get what little money she had. Pearl was saved from this by the coming of the Spanish-American War. The band playing and flag-waving had stirred in Hart a sense of patriotism that he probably never knew he had. He enlisted to fight the Spaniards. When the war ended, Hart returned to Pearl, but she was tired of his conniving ways. She told him that she was through with him once and for all.

In her middle twenties, Pearl began to feel a distinct and bitter resentment toward a society that branded her a woman of sin, a society that refused to recognize her as an equal or to treat her as she wanted to be treated. Unable to find some of the real excitement she craved in the West, she decided to make some of her own. Besides, it would be just desserts for those who thought they were so high-and-mighty.

Soon came the incident which rocked Arizona back on its heels and sent the old-timers into fits of glee.

On the morning of May 30, 1899, the Benson stage to

the Globe mining camp had slowed down on the up-grade through Cane Springs Canyon. Suddenly the startled passengers and disbelieving driver heard the words: "Hands up!"

Around the curve appeared two men, one a very small person, the other of medium build. One of them carried a .38 caliber revolver, the other a heavy .45. Was it all an act? Who would be performing the almost ancient art of stage holdups this day and age? Jesse James was dead but not forgotten. The menacing pistols told the passengers it was no joke. They hurriedly and somewhat nervously climbed down from the stagecoach for the in-spection they expected. The little fellow dismounted and rifled their pockets. After the bold robbery, the pas-sengers discussed the appearance of the one robber.

"Why, he must have been only fifteen years old," said one of them.

"Less, I'd say, more'n likely he was twelve," put in an-other.

In any event, they all agreed that the man who had led such a youngster into a life of crime ought to be hanged, and quickly.

Yes, the supposed boy was Pearl Hart. That spring at Camp Mammoth she had become acquainted with a prospector named Joe Boot. When that camp suddenly closed down, the two of them found they were out of work. To make matters worse, Pearl received word that her mother had moved to Toledo, Ohio, and that she was very ill. Pearl must come at once if she wanted to see her mother alive. Pearl was desperate. She and Joe Boot tried to work worn-out claims, but to no avail.

Joe Boot argued that they should rob the Globe stage. Why not? he wanted to know. It was about the only thing the two could rob without additional assistance or elaborate plans. Both Pearl and Joe recalled reading the stage-holdup exploits of Jesse James and Sam Bass. The idea began to appeal to them. The people who rode the stage between Globe and Riverside could afford to lose what valuables they had with them, and Pearl could put her share of the loot to a good purpose.

The sound of the stage driver's bullwhip echoed in the distance, leaving the lady stage robber and her friend in the middle of the road, figuring out what to do next. They had not carefully planned this robbery; it had been an impulsive deed. They had no idea of a getaway route or actually what to do next. They had committed a serious crime, all the time acting in a careless manner, as though the whole incident was a mere lark.

Why Pearl Hart and Joe Boot didn't put as much distance between themselves and the scene of the holdup remains a mystery. Instead of doing so, they decided to hide out in the mountainous, wooden terrain in Cane Springs Canyon. Like the dreaded Oregon outlaw Harry Tracy they preferred to hide in the dense jungles, and like Tracy, knew less of the topography than anyone. But again the stories of the lurid dime thrillers filled their minds. Why, they threw off pursuit so easy it was laughable. They could do the same by wading in shallow streams and doubling back on their trail, or by creating similar maneuvers to baffle the bloodhounds and the officers who were sure to follow the news of the unthought-of robbery.

The remainder of the holdup day was spent crossing canyons and creeks and backtracking on their trail. They took as much sport in their work as some juveniles in the game of hare-and-hound. The entire area was so unfamiliar to them that by evening they were right back where they started, only a half-mile from the scene of the holdup. The next day Pearl and Joe rode their horses into Riverside and hobbled them in some brush. They then slept for several hours.

It no longer was a secret that the boy robber actually was Pearl Hart. All railroad depots and roads were being carefully guarded, and special groups were out searching the vicinity for the two robbers. After several days of riding through the woods and hiding in deserted buildings or haystacks, the two fugitives were less than ten miles from the scene of the robbery. It seems ridiculous, but such was the case. We will recall a similar incident about the Younger brothers and the Jameses after the Northfield, Minnesota, fiasco. Their Minnesota guide slain, the robbers rode in circles and covered less than fifty miles in ten days. So it was with Pearl Hart and Joe Boot.

The following day it rained. The two robbers carelessly rode the mountain trails, leaving an easy trail of their horses' feet. Pearl and Joe slept for several hours in a cactus clump in the foothills, and shortly after dawn, the excited yells of a nearby posse informed Sheriff Truman of Pinal County that their quarry had been sighted. The next thing Pearl and Joe knew they were looking into the black muzzles of cocked Winchesters.

They hadn't been able to spend a dime of the stolen money.

This last stage robbery in Arizona set a precedent of its own, for old-time outlaws never used women in their operations, and no record has been found other than Pearl Hart of a woman stage robber. It also created much talk among those who had practiced this art of robbery, inasmuch as the whole scheme lacked even an iota of organization or resourcefulness. No doubt many of the ex-outlaws got a big laugh out of it, if nothing else.

To the general public, however, a stagecoach robbery was something romantic and daring, especially at this late date. In fact, Pearl Hart became something of a celebrity over it. It was an asset she had long hoped for, yet never dreamed of having. The whole affair turned out fine for her, even though she was caught and had never spent any of the stolen money. If Pearl could have thrown off the shackles of the law at this particular time, she could have made a small fortune by making personal appearances and selling photographs and autographs.

Pearl was pleasant with her visitors, especially the reporters. Having herself been on the midway in Chicago, she knew what the public wanted. She spoke with the accent of the West, and anyone learning she was a Canadian could hardly believe it and thought it was a whim on her part. The dime novels and the cheap melodrama of the times had inspired in the general public a keen and earnest desire to meet up with an actual criminal, to say nothing of a modern-day stage robber. The eastern papers built Pearl up so much that people began to think another Belle Starr was in the making, but fortunately the deception did not go that far.

To the delight of most Arizonians, the prisoner was moved about the state a great deal by the authorities. Pearl was allowed to speak freely with visitors, and it appeared as though some dignitary had come to town rather than a common stage robber. Pearl was ready at all times to don her boy's costume and to pose with empty rifles and six-guns. She was taken from Benson to Florence by a circuitous route with stops, mainly at Tucson and Casa Grande. So much attention was given the prisoner at Tucson that she requested the crowd be sent away.

"They look at me like I'm some kind of caged animal or a freak!" she cried. "I wonder how they'd act in front of my loaded .45!"

None offered to try.

In June her trial was held at Tucson. She was subsequently sentenced to serve five years in the territorial prison at Yuma, since moved to Florence, Arizona. She entered the bleak walls of the prison, known as The Hell Hole, as convict #1559 on November 18, 1899. Joe Boot was sentenced to serve seven years in the same prison as convict #1558.

Pearl Hart was the first woman prisoner at Yuma, and this fact posed a delicate problem for the officials of the prison. They set aside an exclusive place for her to live and assigned light work to her. In fact, Pearl was better off inside the prison walls than she had been on the outside.

The prison guards were most kind to Pearl and catered to her every whim. But she was clever enough not to use her sex charms to suggest a means of escape or for having special favors bestowed upon her. Pearl's presence became a disruptive matter for the prison, and to many of the female-starved felons she became an angel; others would have sexually attacked her at the first opportunity.

Pearl was kept away from the white prisoners and most of her contacts were Mexicans or Indians, people who cared little or nothing about a white woman. She also tried another trick: she took up praying and pretended to become very religious. She asked for the Bible and other religious books to read. Of course, she knew all this pertinent information would leak out and appear in the eastern newspapers, as well as in the local journals.

It is said that Pearl took another convict into her confidence in an attempt to escape from the prison.

"The beef wagon comes in each Saturday," she told the man, "and it is always covered with tarpaulins. As the wagon is leaving, we can climb onto the wagon, and hide under the tarps."

At the opportune time Pearl and her fellow prisoner did as she had suggested. However, just as the man hid himself under the tarp she made some excuse to return to her cell for some item she had forgotten. As she did so, the wagon pulled away. It was not long before the wagon was stopped and searched and the bewildered convict was soon back in his cell. You guessed it. Pearl had told the guards of the man's attempted escape, thus gaining more points in her favor. From all I have been able to determine I believe this story is a figment of someone's imagination.

Pearl did not have long to wait for the effects of her strategy to become manifest. The local citizens of Yuma began to complain to the warden of the prison that such a hellhole was no fit place for a white woman. Besides, it was plain to see that she had completely reformed. As a matter of fact, in less than two years, even the prison staff members were backing Pearl in her pleas for a pardon. Soon the governor of Arizona saw that he must take personal action on the matter. He granted Pearl a pardon, and on December 15, 1902, she was discharged from the Yuma prison. She started at once for Ohio to see her ailing mother.

In those prison years the celebrity status which had been Pearl's still remained. At El Paso, Texas, a crowd greeted her at the station, morbid people eager for a glance at the lady outlaw, a stage robber at that, the last to be heard of in this country. As far as Stillwater, Minnesota, her name traveled and reached Cole Younger, notorious train and stage robber. Cole smiled upon learning of the publicity being bestowed upon the frail Pearl Hart.

"I know what you mean," Cole told his friends. "My brothers and I had the same trouble when we were captured many years ago. People are funny and will travel miles to see an outlaw, dead or alive. Why, when Jesse James was laid out at Kearney, Missouri, so many people came, even in the rain, that one would have thought the President of the United States had arrived."

At El Paso a young man-about-town tried to rush Pearl off her feet. He wined and dined her for several nights and then tried to get real affectionate. Pearl bushed him off with a warning glance and a statement that she had promised to go straight and to leave all men alone. She told the man that she had taken this oath on the Bible and a crucifix while in Yuma prison. The young man, cowed into an unknown embarrassment, did not bother Pearl again.

Pearl Hart went to the East Coast, where she gave detailed interviews with newspapers and magazines, describing the terrible conditions she had experienced in the prison at Yuma. The publicity again brought her into the limelight. Offers to appear in a play were accepted by Pearl and it was called *Pearl Hart, Girl Bandit*. However, the notoriety soon wore off when the public lost interest in Pearl.

No one seems to know what happened to Pearl Hart. It is said that she appeared in the Buffalo Bill Wild West Show when it stopped off at Yuma, but this has never been verified. And of course, like it always has been said of such characters as Pearl, many swore she started a fancy bawdy house in Mexico.

It was just as well, for her dubious fame was now established, and should she again try the art of stagecoach robbery, she might have destroyed the legend she had built and even perhaps be laughed to scorn.

Except for a few to follow—Harry Tracy and Henry Starr, for instance—the Old West was dead, insofar as the daring holdups were concerned. The dime novel had lost its appeal and had been cast into obscurity by this time; a new era of criminals was being born: those of the city, the gangsters and mobsters who were to run rampant for many years.

So into the pages of the gun-blazing West goes Pearl Hart, woman stage robber and vaudeville performer deluxe.

5. ✓

Annie Oakley: Spirit Gun of the Prairie

"Phoebe! Phoebe! Wait up! We got all day to get that Thanksgiving turkey," cried a young lad, trying his best to keep up with the spindly teenage girl far to the front of him.

"C'mon, Tom, we must get back before dark."

The girl waited for her companion. She carried an old muzzle-loading rifle that seemed taller than she was, a weapon she seemed hardly the person to be carrying.

Here, in 1875, in the swamplands of Ohio, in Darke County, near Cincinnati, turkeys abounded and were part of the family menu. As in the case of many frontier families, it was the duty of the young people to furnish the meat for the family meals.

"Phoebe, there's a big tom jaunting about. Get him."

"Tom, I'm ashamed of you. He's walking. I cannot shoot him unless he is in flight. Throw something at him."

The boy picked up a stone and sailed it toward the unsuspecting turkey. With a shrill, the bird took to the air. At the same time the girl's musket roared and the bird fell to the ground.

"Got him!" cried the boy, dashing up to get the turkey. "Did it again, Phoebe." Tom grinned. "You took his head off."

Sure enough, the bird had been decapitated as though he had been placed on the chopping block.

Who was this young girl, whose name became synonymous with expert rifle and shotgun marksmanship over a hundred years ago, and still symbolizes this art today?

She was Phoebe Annie Moses, born on August 13, 1860, in a one-room cabin near Greenville, Ohio, the fifth child of Jacob and Susan Moses. In 1866 her father died after terriblé exposure to a raging blizzard. Mrs. Moses remarried, but the marriage was brief, for her second husband passed away after the birth of a daughter.

Annie, as her family called her, was delegated to provide meat for the family table. In short order she became an expert shot, always shooting squirrels in the eye and birds on the wing, usually in the head, so as not to spoil the meat. In connection with her hunting, she supplied game to the local store at Greenville, in an effort to reduce the family mortgage.

One day Mrs. Crawford Eddington, wife of the superintendent of the Darke County poor house, paid the Moses cabin a visit.

"Phoebe, would you like to come to the farm and help us? I could repay you by teaching you to sew and to stitch and whatever else I could do," she told the young girl.

"I reckon that would be just fine, sure would help out," replied the nine-year-old Phoebe Moses.

And so it was. The widow Moses was appointed the district nurse of the county. This scattered the children in all directions. Some went to live with neighbors, others were married and had moved to adjacent towns.

Annie remained at the county home for two years, bearing the brunt of excessive labor and jeers from the other children on account of her name. The poor child was slight in build, hardly five feet tall and weighed less than a hundred pounds. The other children would call her Moses Poses and kept up this ridicule until she could stand it no longer. Annie then went to work for another family nearby. She was made to work like a slave and was beaten daily. Finally she ran way. She trudged forty miles through the mountains and prairies before she reached her home. There she learned her mother had again remarried, this time to a man named Joseph Shaw, a poor man and a Civil War veteran.

"My God, Phoebe," cried her mother, "you're skin and bones!"

"Yep, Ma, they worked the tar outta me, but I feel all right, I guess. I'm darlgoned mad, though. They'd call me Moses Poses all the time. It got so I could hear it in my sleep."

So bitter was her hatred for this singsong name that Annie finally changed her name to Mozee, taken from the name of a onetime small suburb of Cincinnati, Ohio. She even changed all the legal records to the name Mozee, as well as placing this name on the tombstones of her family. She never forgave her brother John, who lived by the name of Moses.

By the time Annie arrived home, her older sisters, Sarah Ellen, Elizabeth, and Lyda, had married, leaving only the smaller children at the cabin. Again it became Annie's duty to supply the family with food and to try and reduce the mortgage debt on the sorry-looking homestead.

She did not take long in learning the habits of the animals and the birds in the area. She would trap rabbits and other small game in figure-four traps made with a snare of stout twine. What she loved most was the old cap-and-ball percussion rifle which her father had brought to Ohio from Pennsylvania. She felt it was part of her as she raised the rifle to her shoulder and took aim at some imaginary target. She polished the stock and the barrel until it shone like a mirror.

The heavily wooded areas near the Moses homestead furnished ample space for her to practice and to trap her animals. She became so expert with the rifle it was uncanny. One day as she walked through the woods with her neighbor friend, Tom Walsh, she saw a small bird resting on the top of a tree.

"Tom, think I can hit that bird?"

"Wal," drawled Tom in a voice tone much like that of Annie's, not harsh, not soft, but in between. Not like what Byron said, "Thine voice is music to my ears." It also carried the midwestern-brogue accent.

"Betcha a nickel I can. And I'll hit it in the head."

"Wow, Annie, that's a big order. Fire away, you're on."

The big muzzle loader roared. The bird pitched forward, wings outstretched. When Annie saw that, she knew she had hit the bird in the head, and such proved to be the case.

"Remind me never to bet with you again," said Tom, grinning.

Annie finally did pay off the family mortgage by selling pelts to a trapper named Frenchy LaMonte and game to Charles Katenberger, who sold it to the fine hotels in Cincinnati.

"Charlie, it never ceases to amaze me that all the birds, squirrels, and rabbits you bring me are shot square in the head," the one hotel manager told Katenberger. "Who is this genius marksman?"

"Annie Moses, from over Greenville way," was the reply.

The hotel proprietor thought Katenberger had said, "Andy," and for a long time these feats never were connected to a girl, Annie Moses.

"Ma, here's your Thanksgiving turkey," Annie said as she dropped the plump bird on the kitchen table.

"Annie, you got a letter from Cincinnati today."

"Huh! Who'd write to me?"

The letter was from her sister Lyda, asking her to come to Cincinnati for a visit. It was the break that brought Annie to the attention of the people. Her sister and her brother-in-law took Annie to see the sights of the big city. What intrigued the visitor most was the shooting galleries, in those days a part of most large cities. Her brother-in-law was amazed at the way she would clear the boards of the targets, moving, dangling, standing still, without a miss.

"Good Lord, Annie, where did you learn to shoot like that?"

"Back home, in the woods and 'round."

He was so enthusiastic that he yelled right then and there, "Folks, this is my sister-in-law. I'll bet she can outshoot the great Frank Butler."

Now, everyone there knew who Frank Butler was, Annie did not. They knew he was an expert marksman and trick shooter with his own vaudeville show. Perhaps none of them knew that he was born Frank E. Butler in Ireland, in 1850; like Annie, he had come from a destitute family and had to work when he was a mere child. When he was about eight years old, he was placed in the care of a mean and vicious aunt, never seeing his parents again.

Frank Butler was a likable kid. When he ran away from his aunt's place, he hiked to the seacoast, where he talked a kindly captain into taking him to America. Since Frank had not a shilling, he was taken on the ship as a galley boy, peeling potatoes for his fare and his keep.

In America Frank Butler tried all sorts of jobs, from selling newspapers to working on a fishing vessel. He loved best to trudge the outdoors, to breathe in the fresh air, and to enjoy the sunshine. One day he managed to buy an old broken-down Spencer rifle from a Civil War veteran. Like Annie, as soon as he touched the rifle, he knew what he was meant for. It did not take Frank long to have the old rifle working like a charm. He made a little extra change by challenging men who thought they were better shots, usually winning every match.

Naturally, Frank came to the attention of the owners of a stock company, who realized that expert shooting was their biggest drawing card along their routes. Besides, Frank Butler was a handsome, well-built young man, whose appearance would be a definite asset to his ability to throw a coin into the air and hit it with a rifle bullet.

From 1870 to 1875, Butler was considered the best marksman in the country, with either rifle or revolver. No matter where he went, someone always challenged this ability, just like the old fast-draw gunslingers were challenged to shoot-outs. And Frank had such a pleasant disposition that his opponents went away liking him, not worrying much about the fact that he had beaten them handily. Frank also had an assistant named Billy Graham and it was under the name of Butler & Graham that they took their show around the country.

Like the modern-day movie star or rock singer, Frank was besieged by women of all types, naturally because of his good looks. But Butler did not trust women. His personal experience with his mother and his aunt had been enough trouble for him from that source. He once said, "I think that in this otherwise-well-run world, women seem to be a bad mistake."

That Thanksgiving Day of 1875 found Butler and Graham in Cincinnati, showing their version of *Uncle Tom's Cabin,* when the challenge to compete with Annie Mozee was sent to Butler. Jack Frost, the owner of a local hotel, bet fifty dollars that little Phoebe could outshoot Frank Butler. Of course, the bet was accepted, as expected, and many others were also placed by the citizens of the town.

Early on the morning of the shooting match, Jack Frost drove up in a buckboard, accompanied by Annie Mozee and her sister, Lyda, to a spot called Shooter's Hill. Soon after, another such vehicle drew up. The driver was the tall, handsome Frank Butler, eyes steady and clear, ready to do his act.

"Well, Frost, my opposition here yet?" he asked.

"Yep, ahead of you, 'smatter o' fact. Let me introduce you to Phoebe Mozee and her sister Lyda."

Butler removed his fancy hat and bowed. He could not believe this frail, tiny girl was going to challenge him, the great Frank Butler, master of the art of marksmanship. He pulled Frost aside.

"Jack, is this some kind of a joke? I thought this was a man named Andy. I feel foolish competing with this little girl."

"You'll be surprised," is all that Frost said.

When the crate of fifty live pigeons had been placed in its proper position, the meet was about to begin. The crowd had grown considerably, and Annie was somewhat taken back by all the interest and confusion generated by a simple shooting match, something she did every day, so to speak. She was nervous.

"Be calm, kid, don't let the people bother you. Just imagine just the two of us are here shooting it out," Butler tried to reassure her.

Annie looked up at him; she liked this kind and gentle man. Now she felt better. Annie was to shoot first.

"Release!" she cried.

The bird flew up. She brought her shotgun to her shoulder, fired, and the bird fell to the ground. She had not forgotten, "swing with the bird, pull the trigger when the target fell right."

"Target dead!" was announced from the scorekeeper.

"Good shooting, little girl, mighty good. I'm gonna have to watch my step with you." Then he yelled, "Release!"

Butler's shotgun roared. The bird fell to the ground. Same announcement from the judges.

They were experts—the tiny girl and the smiling, good-looking Irishman. Each had now fired twenty-four times without a miss. When Butler's last target was released, it quartered to the right. Butler missed. Even though the bird had been hurt, it was counted as a miss since it was not dead.

Annie called for her last bird. The pigeon was released. She swung her gun around, fired, and waited for the announcement.

"Dead!" came the cry from the safety pit.

Little Phoebe Annie Moses (now Mozee) had beaten the great Frank Butler. Some people could not believe their eyes. For a long time thereafter the match was the subject of conversation in Darke County and elsewhere.

"Miss Annie, that was some shooting." Butler smiled. "I'd be mighty pleased to take you and your sister to dinner if you'd like."

"But my husband is expecting supper at home," stammered Louise.

"Heck, bring him along, too."

It was a milestone for poor Annie, who had never eaten in a restaurant in her life, nor had been waited on by anyone. It turned out to be a splendid day for all concerned, and when Butler left them, he said, "Here's a few tickets for the show, front-row seats. I'd 'preciate it if you'd come."

Would they! It was another first for the poor folks from the swamplands around Greenville, Ohio.

The following day the Butler & Graham Show moved onward, leaving Annie to settle back down in the little cabin she called home. Some weeks later the mule-riding postman brought Annie a letter, the second she had received in her life. It was from Frank Butler. He explained that his dog missed her and wanted to know how she was. One last letter said that the show was coming back to Ohio in a short while and that she should be ready to marry him. She thought it was a good idea and a fine proposal.

Frank Butler did return to Ohio, but Billy Graham was not with him. Frank explained that his partner had become ill, thus being forced to leave the show. But on June 22, 1876, Frank Butler and Phoebe Annie Mozee were married.

Buffalo Tom Vernon, whose parents had been hanged by the vigilantes in Carbon County, Wyoming, on the Sweetwater, told me that so far as he knew Annie could read and write when she married Butler. Buffalo Tom had been hired by Buffalo Bill, along with a group of Sioux Indians, to perform in his show. However, since Buffalo Tom was only fifteen at the time, Annie was appointed his guardian until he had reached the age of twenty-one.

Some said that she could neither read nor write, that Frank taught her the education she had been denied as a child. This does sound reasonable in light of her early life. Expert with the needle as with the gun, she fashioned her own costumes in their dressing room while Frank read to her.

He also taught her how to toss glass balls into the air and he would break them with pistol. In turn, she was also soon doing the same trick shooting. Her first appearance in this capacity found the audience snickering when she missed the first shot and the glass ball broke on the stage floor.

"Confidence, Annie, you can break these balls with no problem," Frank assured her.

Frank threw another glass ball into the air. The rifle cracked and the ball shattered. A roar of approval went through the audience.

"Since you're my partner now, Annie, we've got to think of a suitable name for you. Annie Mozee does not have a tongue-twisting effect. How about Annie Oakley?"

And so the name Oakley was born. Thereafter, the show was known as Butler & Oakley. Where Frank got the name is a mystery no one will ever know. Buffalo Tom was also unable to tell me. Maybe it was his mother's maiden name or the name of some place in Ireland.

One day Annie was approached by the manager of the Sells Brothers Circus, offering them a spot in his show. It was accepted and in 1884 they became part of that show. However, now Annie Oakley was the main attraction since Frank chose to become her manager. During their stay with the Sells Brothers Circus Frank devised a plan where Annie and others would riddle targets while racing by on their charging mounts.

Expecting large crowds in New Orleans, because of the World's Fair being held there, the Sells Brothers moved their circus to that point. However, because of the cold and drizzle most of the time, the move was a bad one. At the same time, Buffalo Bill Cody and his Mountain and Prairie Exhibition moved to New Orleans, dreaming of the huge crowds that would attend the fair.

While in New Orleans Frank and Annie were approached by Major Burke, publicity agent for the Cody show, and offered a job in their attraction. Annie gave Burke a demonstration of her skill, much to his delight and surprise and to the amazement of the employees of the show, many of whom were Indians. Burke told them to meet the show, now under the name of Buffalo Bill's Wild West Show, in April 1885 in Louisville, Kentucky.

Again, Frank placed himself in the background, content on dismissing his own fine reputation for the sake of Annie. He assisted her at times and managed the act, but all the posters read ANNIE OAKLEY.

She was billed as being the greatest woman marksman in the world in an exhibition of skill with the rifle, shotgun, and pistol. No one doubted the statement in the least. Annie performed the same act for every show, in every state or city the Wild West troupe traveled to throughout the country and the world. Her entrance to the arena would be announced by the rolling of drums as she raced into the center of the ring on a beautiful palomino and blasted impossible targets at will. A mounted cowboy would ride in front of her, tossing targets into the air, with Annie shattering them with ease. She would then leap from her pony, race to a table where Frank stood, waiting to toss glass balls into the air. Frank would toss two, then three, all being broken before they touched the ground. She even went so far as to fire over her shoulder at a target which Frank held, using a gleaming Bowie knife as a mirror. She never missed.

I asked Buffalo Tom Vernon about the origin of the Annie Oakley free pass to performances of many kinds. He told me that Frank would stand some fifty feet with a playing card in his hand and Annie would shoot through the spots on the card, usually one with five numbers. This card brought about the idea of the Annie Oakley pass.

Others tried to get into the act with phony tricks of

many sorts. Frank Butler loved to expose such tactics. One such fraud was the matter of shooting out the flame on lighted candles placed against a board. All the bullet had to do was hit the board and the vibration would extinguish the flame. The shooting of ashes from cigar or cigarette was simply done by placing a long pin through the cigar or cigarette. As soon as the shot was fired, the person holding such between his teeth merely would touch the pin with his teeth, causing the ashes to fall to the ground, as though they had been shot off.

In 1885 Nate Salisbury, Cody's partner, convinced Chief Sitting Bull and some of his Sioux warriors to join the show. When Sitting Bull appeared in the area, he was booed because many of the people in the audience remembered the Battle of the Little Big Horn and the destruction of Custer and his men. Deeply hurt and angry, the chief started for the exit just when the announcement of Annie Oakley's act was called. She repeated her now famous act, much to the delight and satisfaction of Sitting Bull, who followed Annie to her tent. No doubt Major Burke had a hand in what the chief did next; it was good publicity. The old Sioux warrior proclaimed Annie his adopted daughter and dubbed her Little Sure Shot.

The Buffalo Bill Show played to packed houses in Madison Square Garden, New York, and in other large cities throughout the United States and Canada. Buffalo Tom also told me of one incident in the life of Annie which brought tears to his eyes. He said that one day Annie passed an orphanage and saw the kids peering through the iron fence. Never forgetting her own childhood days of privation, Annie asked that all the orphans be allowed to attend the show. They did . . . fifty of them. The habit became a regular one. Whenever they were in a city which had an orphanage, Annie always saw to it that all the children saw at least one of her shows.

In 1887 the show sailed to England, where it camped on the Exhibition Grounds in London. Publicity man John Burke kept the names of the stars before the hungry public. Posters were plastered all over London, displaying pictures of Annie, Buffalo Bill, Sitting Bull, and others. He did a good job.

Royalty from everywhere attended a special showing for their group. Edward, Prince of Wales, and Princess Alexandra were there, along with the King of Denmark, the King of Saxony, the King and Queen of Belgium, the King of Greece, the Crown Prince of Austria, Grand Duke Michael of Russia, and the Crown Prince and Princess of Germany. Several of the members of royalty asked to be allowed to ride in the Deadwood Stage; of course, the request was granted.

Grand Duke Michael of Russia, himself a fair marksman, asked for a shooting match with Annie. Buffalo Bill was worried.

"Frank, what if she accepts and beats him, won't that look bad for us?"

"Of course not, he'd enjoy it either way."

Although a good marksman, the duke was no match for Annie. He broke thirty-five of the glass balls; Annie broke forty-seven, out of a possible fifty.

In Germany the Kaiser failed to show for the cigarette-in-the-mouth trick shot. However, after secretly witnessing Annie's prowess with rifle and pistol, he strode forth and asked to see her. It was agreed. There stood the Kaiser, ruler of Germany, fifty feet from Annie Oakley, waiting to have a cigarette shot from his mouth. Deadly silence fell over the audience. Annie raised her gun and fired, neatly clipping off the cigarette in the Kaiser's mouth. He was high in his praise for her accomplishments.

After they returned to America, Frank and Annie bought a home in Nutley, New Jersey, where she was able to get some much-needed peace and rest. It was the same old thing. Many famous writers of the day made it their business to pay Annie a visit, among them Will Rogers and Teddy Roosevelt.

The show again reopened in 1899 and played to thrilled audiences everywhere, usually attended by people of high rank in politics.

On October 28, 1901, the show left Charlotte, North Carolina, for one more stand for the season at Danville, Virginia. En route, their train smashed headlong into an express train. It was a terrible accident; fortunately no human life was lost, although some valuable animals were lost. Annie was taken to a hospital and then to her home in Nutley. Annie was partially paralyzed and her hair had turned snow white.

Grim and determined, poor Annie tried for a comeback. There were many operations, many days of pain and sleepless nights. Slowly she recovered and learned to walk with a cane and a leg brace.

In Atlantic City she played the lead part in *The Western Girl*, again seemingly her old self. The audience roared with approval, in spite of her slight limp and her dyed hair. But Frank was concerned about her health; all this was too taxing on her strength.

During World War I Annie and Frank played to many army camps and gave shooting lessons in their spare time. They even joined the staff members at the Carolina Hotel at Pinehurst, where Annie gave shooting lessons and Frank managed the skeet range.

Then in 1921 came the serious auto accident. While en route from Jacksonville, Florida, to Leesburg, the car hit a bad spot in the road and overturned. Annie would never appear before the footlights again.

Besides her injuries, Annie was suffering from pernicious anemia. Sensing that the end was near, she asked to be taken back to Greenville, Ohio. She was bedridden all summer and in the fall her sister Hulda came to wait on her. Her last move was to the big house on Third Street in Greenville.

Her beloved Frank Butler was not with her when the end came. She had insisted that he go on ahead to Florida, that she would meet him there later.

On November 3, 1926, Little Sure Shot passed away in her sleep. Frank refused to eat or sleep after that. Just twenty days later he followed Annie in death. Both are buried in the Brock Cemetery.

The whole world mourned the passing of the valiant

and determined little sharpshooter. She was one of a kind and no one like her will again appear. She will live forever in stories, movies, and television; nevermore will she have to hear the praise she despised, "Moses Poses."

6.

Poker Alice: Gambler

It was unbelievable, this rumor which was spreading around Silver City, New Mexico. Yet anything could happen in the Old West, so the excitement-craved prospectors and white-faced gamblers rushed pell-mell to the Gold Dust Gambling House.

"Let's go!" cried one old sourdough as he hobbled along the dusty street toward the gambling casino. "They say a woman broke the bank at the Gold Dust! This I gotta see!"

This was something undreamed of in those days. A woman seldom visited the gambling houses; yet, they say this one broke the bank and would deal the game herself. No wonder these old fortune hunters and bug-eyed citizens made a rush to the Gold Dust. Even the dust devils whirling crazily in the breeze as they danced down the street were seemingly aware of all the excitement going on in this infant city.

The crowd of mixed humanity filled the gambling house and it was not disappointed in what it saw. Perched high on a stool was a stern-faced, determined woman, later to be dubbed Poker Alice. At that particular time she was the widow of a mining engineer named Frank Duffield, who had been killed a few weeks before in a dynamite explosion. She was destined to become the first and most famous woman gambler of the Old West.

This woman was a born chance-taker and not an emotion reflected on her face. Slow but thorough, she dealt the game without the aid of a helper or lookout, something no sensible faro dealer would do with such an important game.

It was no easy chore, this dealing of faro. One had to be keenly alert at all times, with eyes on all things at all times. The cards were dealt one at a time from a small wooden or metal container. Many bets had to be watched, bets must be paid, and money lost had to be dragged in for the house.

Men struggled to get close to Poker Alice as the evening wore on. Perhaps the novelty of betting against a woman dealer enthralled them, perhaps they were taken in by her beauty. Poker Alice was a small woman, about five foot four, with soft brown hair piled high on her head. Steady gray eyes took in everything in a sweeping glance, and her firm, pointed chin wavered not a bit whether she lost or won.

All attention in the Gold Dust was centered around the table operated by Poker Alice. In later years men were to boast they had bet against the famous woman gambler, Poker Alice Tubbs. The men who pushed and shoved for the privilege of betting against her dropped a lot of money that night. By the time the witching hour came around, Poker Alice had won more than six thousand dollars. In short order the rumor spread throughout the West that a woman with eagle eyes and a steady hand had broken the bank at the Gold Dust and dealt faro like a man. That same evening the legend of Poker Alice was born.

Poker Alice was born Alice Ivers in Devonshire, England, February 17, 1853. She was brought to this country at the age of three by her parents and was later educated at a woman's college in the South. Her father, an English schoolmaster, taught her many things as well. However, at the age of twenty she married Frank Duffield and moved West with him. She was not yet twenty-five years old when she broke the bank at Silver City.

Gambling was nothing new to Alice. She had often visited the gambling casinos with her husband. There she learned the thrill of winning a bet on a turned card. It was only natural she would turn to this trade to earn a living after her husband was killed.

Poker Alice was determined to live up to her reputation. After winning high stakes at the Gold Dust, she took a trip to New York City. She told her friends that a gambler had a "prestige" to uphold and she must dress the part.

Alice made many trips to New York City via stagecoach, steamer, and train, there to spend most of her winnings on beautiful clothes and taking in the sights of the great metropolis. She never ceased to talk about the bright lights, courteous men, and extravagant stage shows of the city. Even in New York her fame went before her. Poker Alice was treated with respect and honor.

She traveled the West in style, always alighting from the stagecoach and announcing that she was the woman who had broken the bank of the Gold Dust Gambling House in Silver City. Such towns as Del Monte, Leadville, Georgetown, and Alamosa catered to her whims. Men flocked to place bets against her.

It was in San Marcia, New Mexico, that she hired out to a local gambling establishment as a faro dealer and house player in the poker games. It was the same thing all over again. Men flocked to see the famous woman gambler and it was here that she was really dubbed Poker Alice.

She had not been in San Marcia very long when she fell in love with a professional gambler named W. W. Tubbs. Alice could have easily married any of the wealthy miners who offered to throw their gold at her feet. Instead, true to her ethics as a square gambler, she married the man she loved.

Their wedding was one of the most elaborate ever seen in that little New Mexico town. Disappointed suitors and elite friends showered them with gifts representing a small fortune. It is said this money was used by them to start their dual career beside the gambling tables.

But sometimes Dame Fortune smiles the other way. Alice and her husband found it difficult to make ends meet and she suggested he return to working for the house at a substantial salary. Even though they won and lost, never amassing a fortune of any size, the fame of Poker Alice always went before them and there were always offers in every town they visited for them to deal the games of chance.

People were fascinated by the steely gray eyes of this woman gambler . . . also by the .38 caliber revolver that hung in a holster at her waist. There is record of her using this revolver twice, once to save the life of the man she loved.

It happened during the early hours of the morning. Tubbs was dealing and Poker Alice was bucking the house game her husband dealt. Suddenly a customer began to dispute over a bet, claiming Tubbs had shortchanged him. Tubbs refused to pay more, stating he had paid the proper amount. The troublemaker cursed and grabbed for his knife. Just then Alice went into action. The .38 snapped from its holster and a sharp report of a shot was heard in the room. The attacker dropped his knife to the table as Alice's shot crashed into his elbow. Not a sign of emotion showed on her rigid face. Someone escorted the wounded man out of the building and the play was resumed as if nothing had happened.

Life planned for Poker Alice to see many things other than the green of the gaming tables. She saw men die in shoot-outs in the street and she saw many people die from disease, always doing her part to try to comfort the victims. Death played a grim role in the lives of the people. Alice witnessed young men die in gun duels at the bar, saw them slump to the floor in a heap. It was a time when men dug deep for gold, shallow for graves.

In Deadwood, South Dakota, the former stomping

grounds of Wild Bill Hickok, her husband became seriously ill. All during his illness she refused to work the gaming tables, remaining ever at his side. When the end came and the Grim Reaper turned up the losing card for Tubbs, it is not known whether Alice went to pieces or took the verdict like a good loser. At any rate, when she again appeared in public life, she showed no emotion, nor did she speak about her husband.

Poker Alice followed one strict rule and perhaps it helped her to forget some of the troubles that had befallen her. Every large winning was followed by a trip to New York City. When she returned, she was laden down with garments of the latest fashion, always remarking that a gambler must be well dressed. Some people said her expensive clothes sometimes were a source of income for her when she was broke.

During the winter of 1891 Poker Alice and several miners crossed the Colorado Rockies and stumbled into the little town of Jimtown, sometimes called Creede, since that was the name of the railroad way station. None of the few residents recognized her as a woman dressed in men's clothing, nor did they when she began cutting down trees for her cabin. Alice knew that when the spring weather arrived, miners by the thousands would flock into the area. They did come, and it was not long before Poker Alice had to add to the size of her gambling establishment.

It was also in Jimtown that Poker Alice saw the body of Bob Ford, the killer of Jesse James, after he had been shot by Edward O'Kelley, a good-for-nothing, roustabout town character. She had known Bob Ford there and had often listened to him tell the story that his brother Charley (deceased) had been responsible for the death of Jesse James. However, there is too much proof pointing to the fact that Bob Ford himself shot the famous Missouri outlaw. When the big rush for the Creede-area goldfields opened up, both O'Kelley and Ford had come there from Pueblo, Colorado.

Another actor in the drama about to unfold was Jefferson Randolph "Soapy" Smith. He took over Jimtown, appointing his brother-in-law, John Light, marshal. Smith owned and operated the Orleans Club on the east side of the canyon, and woe betide any sucker who thought he had a chance to win anything in Soapy's place. It was common knowledge that every game in the place was fixed. There were various games: a faro bank, bird cage, roulette, chuck-a-luck, and stud poker, all as crooked as a ram's horn.

The other two gambling emporiums in Jimtown were Ford's Omaha Club and the Gunnison Club and Exchange. Smith wanted the other owners to accept his methods, but they refused to go along with his proposition to fix their games.

The Smith gang went to work on the Gunnison place first. Each night they would go into the place as gamblers and then start a row. Eventually there was the killing of Red McGune, one of the owners, who always tended bar. However, in the case of Bob Ford, the Smith gang was afraid to start anything because they knew he was a dead shot and swift on the draw, not afraid of anything. Consequently, they confined their activities to sending him letters written in chicken blood. These warning letters, signed "Committee," warned Ford that if he did not close and get out of town he would get the same treatment he had given Jesse James.

One night Ford got liquored up, leaped on his pony, and rode up and down the street. He stopped in front of the free-and-easy house referred to as the Central Theatre. There he made a speech to the crowd that had gathered, telling there was a certain element in town writing him unsigned letters and threatening to bump him off. Ford said if there was any one man in town who cared to shoot it out with him, he would be happy to oblige. He would meet anyone interested on the mesa (west of the lower part of Jimtown). By that time the first electric lights had come to Amethyst Street and Ford pulled out his gun and shot out a light some hundred feet away, as a demonstration of his skill. After this, Smith realized that Ford was a dangerous man to fool around with.

Soapy Smith was smart enough to get someone to do his killings for him. Around his saloon Edward O'Kelley regularly looked for free drinks or odd jobs, and Smith picked him as a likely prospect, since he knew that O'Kelley hated Ford because Ford had embarrassed him in front of his friends in a Pueblo honky-tonk. Ford had also whacked him over the head with a pistol and then added insult to injury by taking O'Kelley's pistol with him.

"You'll be known worldwide as the man who killed the man who killed Jesse James!" Smith promised O'Kelley.

A big fire had emptied Willow Gulch of all its buildings. However, some of the wiser inhabitants had erected structures south of Jimtown on what was known as the School Land, which is the present site of Creede, Colorado. Shortly after the fire Bob Ford secured a location on the School Land and had a floor put down. He erected a tent over the flooring and this was to serve as a temporary saloon. His bartender, Joe McKee, on a visit to his mother in Kansas City, did not return in time for the opening, so Ford tended bar himself.

The morning of June 8, 1892, was chilly but clear. Ford was alone in his canvas saloon, cleaning up the place. The Smith gang was aware of it and they encouraged Ed O'Kelley to saunter into the street with a sawed-off shotgun hidden under his coat. Seeing Joe Duval, Ed called him over and asked him to have a drink. Together they walked to Ford's place and O'Kelley shoved Duval through the doorway ahead of him. When Bob turned his head to see who was coming, O'Kelley let him have it with both barrels, shooting him in the throat and almost taking off his head. Poker Alice said she saw Ford's body as it was carried from the saloon.

O'Kelley was arrested, tried in Lake City on July 12, 1892, and sentenced to life imprisonment in the state prison at Canon City. Poor Joe Duval was also tried and given two years for his innocent participation in the murderous deed. Soapy Smith was quite a politician in

Colorado and soon had the gears working to get O'Kelley released, as promised. However, Smith soon forgot about O'Kelley and left for Alaska to try his luck in the gambling dens there. He was killed in Skagway by a man named Frank Reid, an honest citizen who grew tired of Smith's crooked way. In the shoot-out Reid also was killed. O'Kelley finally was released from prison in 1902, mainly through the efforts of his younger brother, Dr. Frank O'Kelley of Missouri. O'Kelley was killed January 13, 1904, in Oklahoma City by a police officer named Joe Burnett after Ed had pulled a gun on the officer.

Norval Jennings, whom I knew for many years, was just a young boy in Jimtown when Ford was killed. He told me he was working in the kitchen in Newman Vidal's log-cabin restaurant near the Ford tent saloon when it happened. He was there when Ford's body was taken from behind the bar. The Creede Elks Lodge now owns this bar, putting it to use in 1937, finishing all but one corner of it in order that the bullet holes can still be seen.

When I asked Jennings how he had come to know Bob Ford, he told me this:

"Well, when the bottom dropped out of Jimtown after the fire and most of the restaurants had closed up, I was out of work and broke. With no place to sleep and no way to get back to Kansas or to Pueblo, it was mighty rough. This was in March and the nights were very cold, sometimes as low as twenty degrees below zero. I went from place to place to get warm by the big potbellied stoves they had in the saloons. On this particular night I walked into Ford's place. There was not a soul in the place except Ford and his bartender. He came up, remarking how cold it was and asking me what I was doing. I told him nothing; he then asked me where I was from and I told him from Minden Mines, Barton County, Missouri. He asked me if I was hungry and I told him that I was. He told me I could help the bartender and could sleep and eat in the kitchen until I found something to do. That is what I did until the fire cleaned out Jimtown. This made business boom at Vidal's restaurant, and I got a job there until I was able to leave Jimtown."

Since this story is about Poker Alice I asked Jennings if she was in Jimtown when Ford was killed.

"Poker Alice may have been there, but she was not there when I was, she was at Cripple Creek when Ford was killed. In a situation like that everyone wants to get into the act; all they do is cloud and confuse the issue so an honest historian gets sidetracked all the time.

"I never saw Ford armed when he was in his place, but he put on his shooting irons whenever he went out. Ford had no children and sold no meals at his place, other than coffee and doughnuts. The two fiddlers were paid nothing except what they could get from the dancers. When I went back there in 1941 and the people found out that I had been there and an eyewitness to all these things, the questions came fast and furious. It was hard for me to leave town, but I enjoyed the attention. I still maintain that if Bob Ford would have been left alone he would have come out all right."

Poker Alice said she left Jimtown soon after the fire had gutted the gulch, moving on to Bachelor, Colorado, but soon she moved on again. It was in Fort Fetterman that she found occasion to pull her .38 for the second time.

One night she was bucking the tiger in a rival gambling house and had lost over a thousand dollars. Somehow Poker Alice did not trust the shifty-eyed dealer, finally deciding he was dealing a crooked game. She drew her .38 and demanded the return of her money. It did not take much persuasion to have the crooked dealer count out eleven one-hundred-dollar bills and return them to her.

Throughout her life Poker Alice knew many famous women as well as famous men. Some of those she counted as friends were Calamity Jane, China Mary, Madame Mustache, and Iowa Bull. By her own admission Poker Alice stated that Deadwood was the toughest mining town she had ever visited. When Deadwood made its sensational strike near what is now the Homestake Mine, Poker Alice was one of the first people there. With her came Kitty Arnold and Calamity Jane. The three of them opened a gambling hall in Deadwood.

She was in Deadwood when Hickok and his self-appointed peace officers ran the town and she witnessed the depredations his men caused. She was one of the first to enter Lewis's Saloon after he had been shot and killed by Jack McCall. She saw the dead man's hand of aces and eights lying under the table where Bill had been seated. She also knew Neil Christy, the man who retrieved the cards and passed them on to his son. Although the cards Hickok had held when he was killed have always simply been referred to as aces and eights, there was the fifth card. Here is an exact identity of these cards as told to me by Christy's son: the ace of diamonds with a heel mark on it; the ace of clubs; the two black eights, clubs and spades, and the queen of hearts with a small drop of Hickok's blood on it.

In Deadwood Poker Alice married a man named George Huckert of Sturgis, South Dakota, but her third husband soon died and she again took the name of Tubbs. When the flame of Deadwood died and the gamblers and miners moved on to other fields, Alice stayed behind. She now made South Dakota her home, and after several extensive trips to New York City and Chicago, she mixed in county and state politics. Many claimed that no office seeker could be elected without her backing.

Some years later, after Alice had been found guilty on a liquor charge and sentenced to a term in prison, Governor Bulow sent Judge Henry Atwater to personally deliver her pardon papers. Alice seldom drank, but she loved to smoke smelly cigars and did so until her death in 1930 at the age of seventy-seven.

I was still a youngster when I met Poker Alice, but I'll never forget the experience or the many stories she related.

7.

Etta Place: She was a Lady

Who was the mysterious Etta Place? The question has for years baffled lawmen and, more recently, researchers. Even the efficient Pinkertons were at a loss to determine anything definite about the beautiful lady. Most of what they knew of her came from clues dropped along the Outlaw Trail: her father was an English peer; she had been well-educated; she was a schoolteacher; perhaps she was a prostitute, since she had been known to abide among Fanny Porter's girls; she had known Harry Longabaugh for years, and perhaps they were man and wife, as they often registered as such in hotels and on ships. But finally, all the Pinkertons ever gleaned for certain (and even this was partly in error) was that which even today appears on their files:

NAME: Mrs. Harry Longabaugh. ALIAS: Mrs. Harry A. Place, alias Mrs. Ethel Place, alias Laura Place.

NATIONALITY: American.

OCCUPATION: Unknown, Criminal occupation.

AGE: 27 to 28 years (1906).

HEIGHT: 5 ft. 4 to 5 in.

WEIGHT: 110 to 115 lbs.

BUILD: Medium. COMPLEXION: Medium Dark.

REMARKS: Wears hair high on top of head in a roll from forehead.

The true story of mysterious Etta Place is probably more amazing than even Pinkertons would have suspected, and had they known who the beautiful Siren of the Wild Bunch really was, history might have taken another turn.

The supposition made by Pinkertons that Etta's father was "believed to be an English peer" was, in this instance, quite correct, but knowing the man in reality would not lead one to believe such.

George Ingerfield was a member of the infamous McCarty gang of outlaws, supplying horses and assisting in establishing getaways after spectacular robberies as early as the late 1870s. But George Ingerfield was more than this.

George Ingerfield was the alias of Hon. George Capel, the illegitimate son of the Hon. Arthur Algernon Capel, Sixth Earl of Essex. According to members of the present Capel family, still renowned in England, George Capel was a rebellious youth who, by his frequent misdeeds, created considerable embarrassment for his father in England and was therefore shuffled off to Ireland, where he was given management over certain estates of his step-uncle, Richard Boyle, Ninth Earl of Cork.

George Capel was a fellow at Cambridge with his distant cousins Gilbert Leigh, James Boothby Roche, and with Moreton Frewen, who became his lifelong friend and associate. An ardent fan of the great Irish horse races, Capel became an excellent rider to the hounds, a lover of fine horseflesh (and ladies), and was a member of the unofficial County Cork "sporting society," which was notorious among the upper crust.

For a brief period Capel was a competitor with Moreton Frewen for the attentions of a lovely stage actress named Emilie Charlotte Le Breton, better known to history as Lillie Langtry, the Jersey Lily. Frewen, especially, became very controversial with his remark that "Lilies were made to bed."

During this time George Capel became master of the Kilkennies, Cork, and Meath estates in southern Ireland, owned by his step-uncle, Ninth Earl of Cork, and by Pierce O'Brien Butler of Dunboyne Castle, who had married his aunt, Georgianna Capel.

Capel earned a reputation as a cruel and tyrannical ruler of the Irish tenant farmers to such an extent that he was forced to flee Ireland under threat of assassination. Unable to return to his Essex home and now an outcast, Capel changed his name to George Ingerfield (the Ingerfields being near relatives) and sailed for New York. Not long after his arrival he was joined there by Moreton Frewen and his brother Richard Frewen, and their old Cambridge society of friends including Gilly Leigh, Jim Roche, Charlie Fitzwilliam, and others, all eager to visit the American West.

Richard Frewen had visited the West on prior occasions and was interested in investigating ranching possibilities there; Moreton Frewen had been induced by none other than General Phil Sheridan to do the same. But before going West, the English gentlemen visited the gay nightlife of New York City, taking in the theaters and Delmonico's.

There is strong evidence that George Capel had been West even prior to this occasion in the company of his good friend Lord Dunraven (Wyndham Thomas Wyndham-Quinn), author of the now famous work *The Great Divide*. Dunraven had visited New York in 1869 and came again in the fall of 1871 and remained long enough to explore Yellowstone Park, guided by Buffalo Bill Cody and Texas Jack Omohundro. It is known that during the summer of 1873, George Capel was a member of the Dunraven party which toured the Catskill Mountains and upstate New York as far as Niagra Falls.

In 1876 Capel was with his friend Moreton Frewen in Kansas. Frewen has left an interesting account of their having met Bat Masterson there.

The Frewen brothers had established the 76 Ranch on the Powder River in Wyoming in 1876, and hauling pine logs from the nearby Big Horn Mountains, they constructed a log "castle" on the banks of the river located near what is now Sussex, Wyoming (named in

Rare photo of Belle Starr in her early years.

Belle Starr and her young Indian lover, Blue Duck.

Rose Dunn, "Rose of the Cimarron."

Kate King, child bride of the famed Confederate guerrilla, William Clarke Quantrill.

Etta Place as a child, and at age about 15, her hair cropped short by her father.

Etta at 18, on completing finishing school in Boston, before coming West to join Butch Cassidy and the Wild Bunch. At right, Etta with Pancho Villa's troops in Mexico, around 1914.

From original tintype, rare photo of "Poker Alice" Tubbs, famous woman gambler. Right, Poker Alice smoked a smelly cigar most of the time until her death in 1930.

Rosamond Collection

Roswell, New Mexico, 1885, old stomping grounds for Poker Alice.

Robert Mullin

Charles Rosamond

Rare photo of Cattle Annie, notorious woman bandit of the Indian territory.

Kerry Ross Boren

Laura Bullion, outlaw's sweetheart, who loved Ben Kilpatrick of the Wild Bunch.

Charles Rosamond

Very rare photo of Pearl Hart, 1888, when she attended a girls' school at Lindsay, Ontario.

Stagecoach robber Pearl Hart.

Prison photo of Pearl.

Annie Oakley, greatest of rifle shots, and Sitting Bull, who joined Buffalo Bill's show along with Annie and gave her the name of "Little Sure Shot."

Buffalo Bill himself, star of his own Wild West Show.

honor of the ancestral Frewen home in England), just a few miles east of the infamous K C Ranch (now the small town of Kaycee, Wyoming).

The castle had all the finest trimmings, individual fireplaces in each room, a magnificent rosewood staircase imported from England with a mezzanine gallery overlooking the massive-beamed downstairs hall known as the Ballroom. Here were held frequent balls and parties while a full orchestra played from the mezzanine. The castle had its own fine piano and one of the largest libraries in the West, with ornamental coal-oil lamps with crystal bangles; the Ballroom sported chandeliers.

The list of distinguished guests astounds the imagination: Sir Samuel and Lady Baker, famous African hunters and explorers; Lord Queensberry, whose rules set the standard for boxing; Lord Gordon; Lord Donoughmore; Lord Manners; Lord Mayo; and Lord Lonsdale and his beautiful wife, Lady Grace, sister to Lord Gordon.

Other guests were Owen Wister, author of *The Virginian,* who used Moreton Frewen as the study for his boss of the 76; sixteen-year-old Florenz Ziegfeld, Jr., who came to the 76 to improve his health; Sir Arthur Sullivan of Gilbert and Sullivan fame; and perhaps the most famous guests of all, Lord Randolph and Lady Churchill, the Duke and Duchess of Marlborough.

It was not by accident that the Churchills were invited guests, for Lady Churchill was the former Jenny Jerome of New York, and was a sister of Clara Jerome, the wife of Moreton Frewen. They were also the parents of the illustrious Sir Winston Churchill.

During his frequent forays in New York, George Capel, alias Ingerfield, became enamored of a lovely young aspiring actress of the Place family (whose name is known but will not be revealed due to certain promises of privacy to present members of the Place family), a young and beautiful near relative of the mother of Harry A. Longabaugh—Annie G. Place.

Details of the affair between Capel and Miss Place are sparse, but suffice it to say that Miss Place became pregnant with his child and Capel speedily left for the West, forgetting his obligations. Miss Place, whose mother had died in a tragic house fire when she was young, was escorted out of New York by her father, and in later years she related having spent time at Mont Clare, Pennsylvania, and her illegitimate daughter may well have been born there.

The given name of Etta Place at birth is uncertain, but it is believed that she was named Laura Etta Place, but as the granddaughter of the Sixth Earl of Essex—had her birth and legitimacy been acknowledged—she would have taken her place in history as Lady Laura Etta Capel-Place.

As an infant Etta was raised by relatives in Pennsylvania and New York, her mother having married and moved first to Michigan and finally to Tacoma, Washington. While in New York, Etta's father suddenly and unexplainedly appeared and whisked the girl off on a whirlwind tour of the West, visiting San Francisco and staying at the renowned Palace Hotel. Etta was not more than ten years of age at this time.

For a time, Etta was the guest of Moreton Frewen on the 76 Ranch on the Powder River, and here became a favorite of the cowboys and rustlers who frequented the region.

It had been Moreton Frewen who, in search of new range for his vast herds, had opened up the valley at the base of the Big Horn Mountains and called it Hole-in-the-Wall after the English pub section of Old London, England. George Capel and Lord Lonsdale, the latter being a perpetual favorite of the outlaws, established an operation for Frewen on a branch of the Powder River in the center of Hole-in-the-Wall, which later became the famous Bar C Ranch.

It is interesting to conjecture that Etta Place, at less than ten years of age, may have preceded even Butch Cassidy and the Sundance Kid to this most infamous of outlaw strongholds.

By the age of fifteen, Etta Place was spending her winters in the normal schools of New York and Pennsylvania and summers in the West with her father, usually as a guest of Moreton Frewen in Wyoming, or of Lord Carlisle (another relative of her father's) at his ranch near Monticello, Utah. At the Carlisle Ranch, Etta was known as Etta Carlisle, apparently taking the name of whomever she lived with.

There are those yet who remember young Etta Carlisle, who was frequently escorted to dances by Dan Parker (Cassidy's younger brother), and on one occasion she is remembered for playing the piano in Lord Carlisle's extravagant home, known as the White House, while accompanied by Harry Longabaugh on the clarinet and Robert LeRoy Parker (alias Butch Cassidy) on the mouth organ.

George Capel, alias George Ingerfield, still maintained a lucrative horse-rustling syndicate throughout the Southwest, and frequently his daughter, hair cropped short and dressed in boy's clothing, accompanied him on these forays. She could soon ride and shoot better than most men, and quite apparently preferred the exciting way of life to her more serene eastern pursuits.

But Etta's exciting life abruptly halted when her father was ambushed and killed by one of his disgruntled Irish tenant farmers who had tracked him to a point near Tombstone, Arizona, in about 1892.

At the time of his death, George Ingerfield had in his employ a trusted servant named Emille Pascale, who was tending a herd of horses near El Paso, Texas. Pascale had once been injured in a fall from a horse and walked only with great difficulty; Ingerfield had been his benefactor.

Pascale therefore felt a great debt for his former employer and took the teenage Etta under his care for some time, but eventually he placed her in the more feminine care of a Mexican prostitute in a bordello in San Antonio.

It was at this time that Robert Leroy Parker, alias Cassidy, learned of her plight, and his past friendship for her father and his own religious upbringing (Mormon) encouraged him to take her out of the influence of the bordello and place her with "a good Mormon family" in Utah.

The family that Cassidy chose was that of John Johnson Thayn, a polygamist with seven known wives who resided at Castle Dale, Utah, on the western rim of Robbers Roost. Thayn was a Scotsman, born in Glasgow on November 11, 1825, who had migrated to Utah in 1861. He had served missions for the Mormon church in Canada, England, and the United States, and later became a justice of the peace in the small town of Wellington, Utah, near Price, where he died May 21, 1910.

The second wife of Thayn was Elizabeth Hunt, whom he married on October 25, 1862, in Salt Lake City, and by whom he had six children, among them a daughter, Annie Marie Thayn, born March 30, 1869, in Salt Lake City, a twin of her brother, Edgar Hunt Thayn. It was with this family that Etta Place resided for several years; considered to be a stepsister of Annie Marie's, she was known locally as Ethel Thayn.

On July 24, 1891, Etta was certainly at the Carlisle Ranch near Monticello, Utah, for on that occasion she was escorted to the Pioneer Days dance by two dashing young cavaliers, Dan Parker and Elza Lay. It was at this celebration that Tom Roach, a drunken Texas cowboy of the Carlisle outfit, accidentally shot and killed Mrs. Charles E. Walton, a Mormon lady. Etta was rushed back to the White House by Parker and Lay, fearing incriminations by the Mormon settlers against the Carlisle cowboys, but Lord Carlisle came down in person and extended apologies and the affair was calmed.

In 1893, Cassidy, the Sundance Kid, Lay, and "the boys" took up a collection (probably proceeds from a robbery) and sent Etta Place back East to attend a finishing school, thus removing her from the violent environment of Utah. An opportunity had presented itself when Queen Anne Bassett of Brown's Park was given the opportunity by her father to attend Miss Potter's School for Girls at Boston, Massachusetts. Anne had no intentions of going, however, and according to Anne's sister, Josie Bassett (whom Cassidy was "sparking"), Etta Place went in her stead.

Etta's greatest accomplishment at the school was her frequent outbursts of western euphemisms calculated to entertain her eastern girlfriends, while she labored hard to enjoy the equestrian arts under the formal tutelage of a French riding master. In his absence, Etta would frequently ditch the sidesaddle to ride bareback and astride her mount, displaying her considerable ability at horsemanship by putting on a rodeo. Needless to say, she was on probation most of the two years she attended the school.

Etta Place must have left Miss Potter's School prior to 1895, for on September 6, 1895, she enrolled in State Normal and Training School at Buffalo, New York, under the surname of a Pennsylvania relative with whom she was living in New York at that time. She gave her age as nineteen years (and thus, if correct, she was born about 1876) and her record shows that her studies included advanced German, civil government, English, algebra, geography and map drawing, rhetoric and composition, physiology, botany, zoology, and school law. She graduated with a teacher's certificate in English on June 28, 1898.

After graduation, Cassidy secured a teaching job for Etta at Telluride, Colorado, and Pinkerton records state that she may also have taught school briefly at Denver. Neither could have been for a prolonged period, for she left Telluride one day and rode the long distance alone to join Cassidy at Robbers Roost in search of the more exciting life she preferred.

A clear pattern emerged: Etta Place was Butch's girl. He had saved her from the bordello, saw to her education, and protected her from every threat. There was no doubt that Etta Place was enamored of him, in spite of the fact that he was some ten years her senior. Cassidy had been sentenced to prison on July 4, 1894, and in that year Etta went away to Miss Potter's School in Boston. Cassidy left prison in January 1896, during which time Etta was enrolled in teacher's college in New York, apparently because she could no longer be with Cassidy.

When Cassidy left prison, Etta left school in Buffalo and came West, where she joined him at Robbers Roost. They spent the winter together in a tent on Upper Pasture above Horseshoe Canyon on Badman Trail; Elza Lay and Maud Davis honeymooned in another tent not far away, secluded in the cedars. Sundance was present, too, but not as Etta's paramour, for they never were man and wife, but cousins, and the kid looked upon Etta as a sister, and he as her protector.

Perhaps this is a good place to mention that the Sundance Kid married Annie Marie Thayn in the summer of 1900, and she gave birth to his son in February 1901; at that time the Kid was on his way to South America with Etta Place. Annie Marie was disowned by her family for the marriage, and she moved to the Northwest, where she died in a train accident several years later. Her son, and the son of the Sundance Kid, was raised by foster parents.

The irony of the story of Etta Place from this time forward is that the clues to her situation were always in plain sight for all to see, but few could see beyond the clever smoke screen of her "marriage" to the Sundance Kid. Etta Place is wearing a wedding ring plainly in the photo taken of her with the Kid in New York in February 1901, and also plainly showing is the expensive Tiffany gold watch that Cassidy bought for her at the same time. No one connected the watch with the ring, for they were bought by the same person—Butch Cassidy. There is little doubt that Cassidy and Etta Place were lovers, but more than this, probably man and wife.

There is also evidence that Etta Place gave birth to two daughters in South America, both probably Cassidy's children—one of them certainly. A daughter named Thelma was born in the Chubut Valley not long after the arrival of Etta Place or in about 1903. On June 15, 1905, the second daughter was born, named Flossie Bettie Jane. Señora Blanca de Gerez, Etta's close friend and neighbor at Cholila, Chubut Valley, Argentina (who was living as recently as 1971) , reported:

" . . . The señora [Etta] gave birth to a daughter in that year [1905, following the Río Gallegos bank robbery] and took her north and she did not return for a year. When she came back in about 1907 [1906] she did not have the baby with her and not long after that, all of them left Cholila and did not ever return."

One or both of the small girls were placed in a convent in Buenos Aires, then taken to Santiago, Chile, in 1906 when Cassidy, Longabaugh, and Etta Place were forced to flee from Cholila, this according to a neighbor named George Perry, whose son still resides near Cholila.

The year 1906 appears to have been a year of transition for Etta and her male companions, for in that year she began a love affir with a handsome Scotsman neighbor, John "Jock" Gardner, which ended only when Longabaugh learned of it and threatened to kill Gardner, at which time the Scotsman left promptly for England and never returned. He died at Cong, County Mayo, Ireland, May 4, 1946.

Cassidy, too, was philandering during this period. Señor Francisco Juarez of Buenos Aires presently has in his possession a collection of love letters which Cassidy wrote to a lovely señorita of that city.

Late in 1906, Longabaugh wrote to a friend at Cholila that "tomorrow we leave for San Francisco . . . I do not care to see Cholila ever more. . . ." Cassidy, Longabaugh, Harvey Logan, and Etta Place were together at Santiago, Chile, where Etta had relatives in the embassy, where arrangements were made to take the two girls back to the United States.

Longabaugh and Etta sailed for San Francisco from Santiago with only one of the girls—Bettie, aged about one year—while Thelma, about four, remained with Cassidy at Santiago for a period. In later years she claimed that her father hung a metal tag around her neck, put money in her purse, and placed her in care of a ship's captain and sent her to the States alone.

From San Francisco, Longabaugh and Etta went to Denver, where Etta Place had surgery performed. Pinkertons maintained that this was for appendicitis, but revelations by the youngest daughter in later years proved that the surgery was a follow-up to a cesarean section done when she was born a year previous.

Longabaugh commenced to get drunk in Denver and shot up the ceiling of his hotel room. Pinkertons learned of his presence and he hastily departed for South America. In the meantime Etta Place went with a man called Harvey Logan (not Kid Curry), alias Harley Long, to his ranch on Lance Creek, near Casper, Wyoming.

Eventually the younger girl, Bettie, was given over to a relative of Etta's—a man named Norman E. Weaver—to be raised, while Thelma appears to have remained in the care of Uncle Harv Logan, alias Long.

The events in the life of Etta Place from 1906 until about 1910 are vague, but in the latter year she appeared at the home of Nephi Thayn (e), a brother of Annie Marie Thayn's (former wife of Harry Longabaugh), in the Mormon Colony of Colonia Dublan, Chihuahua, Mexico. Cassidy was living nearby in the home of a friend, George Brown, under the alias of Tod McClamy, while Longabaugh was fighting in the revolution in Nicaragua with a friend, Tracy Richardson, a soldier of fortune. Longabaugh joined Etta at the Thayne home in Dublan in 1911, and at about the same time went to work on the nearby massive ranch of Lord Beresford, of which Nephi Thayne was foreman. Longabaugh assumed the alias Tex McGraph.

In 1912 the Mexican Revolution broke out in earnest and Cassidy, Longabaugh, and Etta all joined Pancho Villa's cause, mostly running guns and ammunition across the border. They were joined briefly in Mexico by George Musgrave of the old Blackjack Ketchum gang, with his wife, Janette Magor, of Baggs, Wyoming. Etta gave her prized Tiffany watch to Janette Magor Musgrave before they departed for South America, and the watch was in the possession of her nephew, Boyd Charter, until his death recently on August 26, 1978.

While Cassidy, Longabaugh, and a friend from early days in Utah—Mike Cassidy—were aiding Villa in robbing trains throughout Mexico and running guns across the border, Etta Place became Villa's "lady general," in charge of training the women soldiers of Villa's army, better known as the *soldaderas*. There exists a photo of Etta taken at this time (about 1914) sporting a rifle, pistols, bandoliers, and still looking beautiful, though now approaching midlife.

Not much is known of her activities other than that she appears to have been well acquainted with both Pancho Villa and the dashing Zapata, and there exists some indication that she may have been the mysterious lady general known among Villa's followers only as Carmen, who showed such daring and courage by riding into the federal troops at the head of her *soldaderas* and holding them in rank until Villa's troops could arrive. In Argentina Etta Place had been known as Red Hawk (for she had dyed her hair red), and Carmen means red in Spanish, or the equivalent thereof.

In 1915 Cassidy visited the 101 Wild West Show at the San Francisco World's Exposition and informed an old friend—Cowboy Joe Marsters—that Etta was at that time living with Sundance in an Indian village near Mexico City.

In about 1919, Etta's daughter Bettie became pregnant at the age of fourteen, and learning of it—although she had not seen her daughter since 1906 or 1907—Etta had the girl brought to her home near Dallas, Texas. The girl gave birth to the child, which died only shortly thereafter of a rare cancer. In 1920, Etta Place was living in Fort Wayne, Indiana, where she had gone to return her daughter to the care of Norman Weaver, and thereafter, to all intents and purposes, disappears forever.

But we are not left without clues. During the 1950s, Queen Anne Bassett Willis was residing at Leeds, Utah, in the house of one of Cassidy's cousins—the McMullins—when she claims that Etta Place visited her. They shared tea and reminiscences.

As late as the 1960s rumors persisted that Etta Place was yet living "with a niece and nephew," well into her nineties.

Perhaps it was true, for as late as 1971, as Etta's daughter Bettie lay dying of cancer in a hospital in the Northwest, she informed her husband that ". . . Mother may still be living. . . . She remarried and may have had other children. . . ."

The final curtain on the life of Etta Place probably drew to a close somewhere in or near Denver, Colorado. Only a few years ago Janette Magor, wife of George Musgrave—returned from South America—died in a rest home in Denver, Colorado. Many thought her to be Etta Place. But the most pertinent information of all was gained from her when she revealed with a smile that her lifelong friend Etta Place had died "not long ago" in the same place. Whether she meant the rest home, or Denver, is uncertain. The important thing is that Etta Place was still around—and perhaps it is only fitting that something mysterious still enshrouds the life—and death—of the always beautiful, always mysterious Etta Place.

8.

Kate King Quantrill: Guerrilla's Bride

The true story of Kate King Quantrill has escaped re-searchers all these years; yet, it was in plain sight all the time. Fortunately this material can now be preserved for the sake of posterity.

On June 6, 1865, 3:45 P.M., a man was dying; at 4:00 P.M. the man on the cot in the Catholic hospital at Louisville, Kentucky, gasped several times and then went limp.

William Clarke Quantrill, the notorious and vicious guerrilla during the Civil War in Missouri was dead. He and a group of men had been surprised in a barn on the Wakefield farm by Captain Edward Terrell near Smiley, Kentucky, and several of Quantrill's men had been killed and their leader was mortally wounded.

First taken to the Wakefield home, Quantrill was later ordered to be hauled in an army wagon to the military hospital in Louisville. Shortly before his death he was taken to the Catholic hospital, where a priest baptized him into the Roman Catholic faith. It is said that Quan-trill gave the priest a thousand dollars in gold. Another such amount, the last he had, Quantrill gave to Kate King Quantrill, his wife. She later went to St. Louis, where, it is reported, she opened a gaudy bawdy house which flourished well.

No one was present at the time the guerrilla chief died

except the priest, a Catholic sister, and Kate. No records indicate that Kate cried or was too upset over Quantrill's death. She never visited the secret grave in the St. John's Catholic Cemetery, now Portland Cemetery, nor did she participate in the removal of some of his bones when W. W. Scott and Quantrill's mother took some of them to his home town at Dover, Ohio, for burial. How many bones actually were buried in an unmarked grave in the Dover cemetery is a moot question, probably none. A small box was buried, no one knows exactly where at this late date. We know for certain that W. W. Scott kept Quantrill's skull at his home for many years.

It was almost certain that Kate was thinking of the warm spring day when she first saw Quantrill near Blue Springs, Missouri, back in 1861. As she stared at his remains, no doubt she recalled she was only thirteen then and not too concerned with events of the Civil War or of the livid tales of John Brown's raids and those of the Kansas Jayhawkers into Missouri. She had heard the name of Quantrill several times while at the dinner table when her parents spoke of him being outlawed in Kansas for some reason she could not remember.

As she skipped along the dusty road from the country schoolhouse she attended, young Kate King saw a horseman riding toward her. She was immediately impressed by his handsome features, his smooth-textured skin, and his poise as he gracefully carried his six-foot-tall body proudly in the saddle. Now, one can well imagine how this same girl, at the age of seventeen, felt as she sat at the bedside of the infamous guerrilla leader, with no one to counsel her.

Quantrill greeted the young girl with his winning smile; she, of course, returned the courtesy, not knowing who the rider was at the time. As the days passed, Quantrill and Kate met secretly at a spring not far from the modest home of her parents, Robert and Malinda King, both God-fearing people. They were parents who wanted the best for their children.

When Robert King learned of the secret riding trips over the countryside by his daughter with William

Quantrill, the outlawed guerrilla, he was furious. Her parents forbade Kate to see him again. Yet she would sneak out at nights to meet her lover in a secret place. Things were fine while Quantrill and his raiders were riding against the federal soldiers in Missouri, but just as soon as he returned to Jackson County, he sought out Kate for companionship.

To escape the terrible wrath of her father's anger, Kate fled to Quantrill's camp for protection. This was in 1863; she was fifteen years old. Some writers appear anxious to throw a dash of extra romance and mystery into this matter by saying that Quantrill kidnapped Kate King. Probably her father originated that story rather than admit publicly that his daughter had eloped with Quantrill. Apparently Kate and her parents were never reconciled. That is what some writers would have the reader believe. Four or five years after the Civil War she returned to the home of her parents in Jackson County. There she built a new home for them; their home had been burned to the ground by federal soldiers during the war. It is also known that she kept house for her brother and her nephew in the same dwelling from 1912 to 1920. It is believed that this same house stands today. I saw it some years back.

Charles Taylor, a prominent member of the Quantrillians, later stated that his chief took Kate to a preacher six miles from their camp, and they were officially married. Taylor further stated that he loaned his horse to Kate for the trip. Therefore, from all evidence at hand, it is easy to assume that Kate King went willingly with Quantrill rather than being kidnapped. Their honeymoon was spent in an abandoned log cabin; this was reported later by the woman who claimed to have been Quantrill's child bride.

The men of Quantrill's command treated Kate kindly. Most of her time with Quantrill was spent in tents near his men during the summers and in wandering from place to place farther south during the cold Missouri winters. Hardly anyone knew she was not a member of the band; consequently, she was never bothered by anyone. She assumed the name of Kate Clarke as a safeguard, in case she was ever captured by federal authorities. By using Quantrill's mother's maiden name—his middle name as well—it would save her much embarrassment if questioned.

When Quantrill was laid up in Jackson County with a bullet wound in the face, Kate asked him why he had attacked the peaceful town of Lawrence, Kansas.

"To capture and kill that damned Jayhawker General Lane, the worst of the lot. I would have burned him at the stake had I caught him, even though my men wanted to publicly hang him in Jackson County," he told her.

Quantrill's retreat into Texas after the Lawrence raid caused dissension in the ranks of the guerrillas inasmuch as others wanted to lead the men, such men as George Todd and Bill Anderson. The final result was that Quantrill lost his command completely and returned to Missouri a broken man.

With the deaths of Anderson and Todd during the raid of General Sterling Price on Westport and Kansas City, Quantrill thought he again might rise as the savior of the Confederacy in Missouri. Here was his chance to regain his popularity by organizing a new command of guerrillas to continue the war.

Sending Kate Clarke Quantrill to St. Louis, he returned to Jackson County to meet some of his old followers at the home of the widow Dupee, in Lafayette County. Some of the guerrillas went to Texas; others rode with Quantrill into Kentucky.

By nature Quantrill was mean and vicious, and he also was a superstitious fatalist. Even his horse seemed to have absorbed some of his mean nature. No other man could handle the animal, for it would kick, bite, and squeal if anyone but Quantrill tended it. Several days before his last fight, one of the guerrillas was shoeing Quantrill's horse, and it became hamstrung because of the struggle it put up during the process. Quantrill was told of the incident and recoiled as though a snake had bitten him.

"That means my work is done. Death is coming. The end is near."

The end did come shortly after that at the fight near Smiley, Kentucky, at the Wakefield farm.

It is a known fact that Kate King Quantrill spent many of the ensuing years in St. Louis and Jackson County, Missouri. She later married a man named Woods, but not much is known of this marriage.

In 1930 an eighty-two-year-old woman died at the Jackson County Old Folks home. Her name was Sarah Head at the time, having been married three times, she said—to Quantrill, Woods, and Head. Only a few confidants knew Sarah was actually Kate King Quantrill, but the world is fortunate to have learned the truth as to what happened to the Civil War child bride of the notorious guerrilla chieftain. Kate kept her secret well while at the home, seemingly happy to sit and dream of the days gone by. Though she was a friendly person, she seldom spoke to anyone, and kept, for the most part, to herself. What a story she could have told had she been so inclined.

Kate was buried in an unmarked grave in the little cemetery at the Jackson County Old Folks Home. It is a shame that she cannot rest near the graves of her parents at Blue Springs.

What about Quantrill? Where did he come from? What really happened to his remains after death? Following is a brief history which will respond to these questions.

It all began in Canal Dover, Ohio (now Dover), when a child called William Clarke Quantrill was born on July 31, 1837, a son of Thomas Henry Quantrill. The father, Dover's first superintendent of schools when the system was organized in 1849, was not to see his son's rise to infamy along the burning borders of Kansas and Missouri; to read of the massacre of citizens of Lawrence, Kansas, or the slaughter of Union soldiers in Missouri. Apologists for the notorious guerrilla have stated all this was done in retaliation for federal acts of torture and the burning of Missouri towns and villages.

Young Quantrill taught school at the age of seventeen in Dover, Brandywine, and other places, but in 1855, at the age of eighteen, he left Dover, never to return. His mother, Caroline Clarke Quantrill, was to see her son's bones thrown to the winds, so to speak, with only bits of them finding a permanent resting place in an unmarked, secret grave near that of his father in Dover.

In 1857 Quantrill went to Kansas with the Beeson-Torrey families, but his venomous nature soon showed itself and he was forced to flee the state because of his thievery and cheating at cards. He went to Utah and Colorado for a time, riding with the military and using card-shark tactics to earn a living. He was soon found out and tossed out to shift for himself.

Quantrill returned to Kansas in 1860, sometimes using the alias of Charley Hart in his dealings. He soon became involved in the slavery and antislavery border wars. When the Civil War broke out, Quantrill associated himself with the South, chiefly because he hated all Kansas with a passion, and because it gave him an opportunity to plunder and kill at will. After one scrape in Kansas he escaped into Missouri and for some months lay low just across the border from Miami County, Kansas. He persuaded four devil-may-care young fellows to join him in robbing the home of a wealthy slaveholder named Morgan Walker, who lived in Jackson County, about ten miles from Independence, Missouri. He then betrayed his associates to the intended victim, and three of them were shot and killed, Quantrill himself killing one of them.

On his return to Miami County he was locked up in jail. Missouri friends came to his rescue and bailed him out, and quickly he joined them beyond the jurisdiction of the Kansas officials. Prior to that Quantrill had openly expressed his sympathy for the Kansas Free-State movement; now he went over to his Missouri comrades and became the leader of that state's most daring proslavery guerrillas. The most successful raids of the Missouri marauders were under the leadership of Quantrill.

But as all things must end, so did the Civil War. At

White River, Arkansas, Quantrill and forty-eight of his men parted company with George Shepherd's men who were going to Texas, Jesse James among them. Quantrill and his own company, Frank James among the men, wearing blue uniforms as a disguise, passed the Union lines into Kentucky. At Houstonville Quantrill decided his men needed fresh mounts. He went to the hotel to chat with the commandant, while his men went about their business of stealing horses. At that point an excited corporal raced into the room, informing that Union soldiers were stealing horses from the corral. The commandant strapped on his revolvers and went dashing from the building, followed by the laughing Quantrill. Quantrill leaped upon a fast mount, shooting the major as he did so; then he and his men raced away from town, giving the rebel yell as they rode.

Early in May Quantrill started for Salt River with William Hulse, John Ross, Clark Hockinsmith, Isaac Hall, Richard Glasscock, Robert Hall, Bud Pence, Allen Parmer, Dave Helton, Lee McMurtry, and Payne Jones. When they were near the post office of Smiley, Kentucky, a terrible rainstorm forced the guerrillas to take refuge in an old barn on the Wakefield farm. A federal cavalry detachment under the command of Captain Edward Terrell, quite by accident, noticed the tracks in the mud which had been left by Quantrill's band as they had turned into the barnyard.

Glasscock was first to see the federals charging at full gallop toward the barn, and it was impossible for the guerrillas to saddle their mounts. Quantrill leaped up from a sound sleep, shouting it was every man for himself. Ross, Hulse, Parmer, Pence, and McMurtry were able to cut their way through the blue ranks, firing right and left as they did so. Quantrill was in the barnyard trying unsuccessfully to mount his spirited steed. He leaped to the back of Hockinsmith's horse, on which both men tried to escape. A volley cut Hockinsmith to pieces. The horse, also hit, leaped into the air, spilling Quantrill into the mud. Jones, Helton, and the Halls raced to the safety of the timber, while Glasscock tried in vain to rescue his leader. Another volley killed him and mortally wounded Quantrill, who was struck by two Spencer rifle balls, one in the hand, the other entering and shattering the collarbone and ranging downward along the spine, paralyzing him from the waist down.

Quantrill was carried to the Wakefield house, conscious enough to grasp the fact that he was dying. The escaping guerrillas had met at Sayers, about twenty miles from the Wakefield farm, and there were given the grave news. It was suggested that they rush the farmhouse to rescue Quantrill. However, the guerrilla chieftain's message ordered them not to make any rescue attempts, for if they did, the federals would burn the Wakefield house to the ground. He also asked them to surrender to the Union authorities in Kentucky. Meanwhile, General I. Palmer, in charge of the Department of Kentucky, feared that Quantrill's men would raid the farmhouse, so he had Quantrill transferred to the military hospital in Louisville. While this was going on, the remainder of Quantrill's band in Kentucky surrendered to Captain C. Young, U.S. Army Regulars, at Samuel's Depot, Nelson County, on July 26, 1865, the later famous Frank James among them.

Reverend Powers, a Catholic priest, buried Quantrill's body in a hidden grave in the St. John's Cemetery. Mr. Scally, the sexton, and his wife, Bridget, were instructed to do all they could to keep the grave site hidden. Mrs. Scally threw her daily wash water onto the level spot to further hide its location from possible grave-robbers and the morbid curious.

The remains of Quantrill probably would have slept in peace had not W. W. Scott, a schoolmate of Quantrill's and editor of the *Dover Iron Valley Reporter*, become interested in what had happened to his boyhood friend. Some time after the Civil War he began to investigate the career of the "Quantrill" mentioned so many times during the war in Missouri. Going to Paola, Kansas, Scott learned from Dover friends who had settled there that the guerrilla chief was the Quantrill from Ohio. The evidence Scott obtained convinced Mrs. Quantrill that the famous guerrilla was her son, so she expressed a desire to visit the place where he had been killed and talk with the folks who had known him.

She went to Nelson and Spencer counties in Kentucky, where she visited and stayed one winter with Sheriff A. D. Pence of Nelson County. Pence had ridden with Quantrill and tried to make the guerrilla's mother as comfortable as possible, as did other members of the old band. But now it was 1887; Quantrill no longer was the dashing hero the Confederacy once thought he was. He was dead and buried and all but forgotten. Mrs. Quantrill, however, became obsessed with what she considered her "hero son," fully expecting the people to treat her as the mother of such a man.

Scott's interest was aroused so much and to such a pitch that he lost no time in arranging another visit to Louisville with Mrs. Quantrill, paying all her bills and introducing her to other friends of her son's. An account of his second trip was given in the following detailed manner:

On Wednesday, Dec. 7, 1887, I visited the St. John's Catholic Cemetery (formerly called Portland), Louisville, Ky., and called on Mrs. Bridget Scally, the widow in charge. I had called on her husband and herself in the spring of 1884, when I was trying to find out what had become of the body of Wm. Clark Quantrill (the guerrilla), who died in Louisville, June 6, '65. Her husband was then confined to his bed, but both told me that they were present when the body was buried; had been in charge of the cemetery all the time, and Mrs. Scally pointed out to me the spot; although there were no signs of a grave. At this second call I found the husband had died, but Mrs. Scally was still in charge. I told her that now I had Mrs. Quantrill with me in the city, that she was anxious to see the grave and to talk with her about her son; and that if she could not remove the bones and place them in the family cemetery in Ohio, she would like to have them taken up and placed in a zinc-lined box.

I took Mrs. Quantrill from the hotel, and herself and Mrs. Scally talked matters over, and Mrs. Scally agreed that the grave might be opened so Mrs. Quantrill could see condition of affairs. Next day, Thursday, Dec. 8, 1887, I went out after dinner and had the grave opened. It was a cloudy, drizzly day and uncomfortable, and Louis Wertz, the employee, did not like to do the work, but I gave Mrs. Scally $2.50 for the privilege, and Wertz a dollar extra. It was 3 P.M. Mrs. Scally pointed out the place, and by spading around a little, the outlines were soon found, and the bones were reached in an hour. They lay in natural position, except top of skull was uppermost, instead of lying on backward. Every vestige of coffin had disappeared except a rotten piece size of a man's hand. His hair had slipped off in a half circle around the skull, and was of a bleached yellow color. A small part of a Government sock was about the boot bones; and some shirt buttons were found. A part of the backbone and ribs were so decayed that they crumbled to pieces, but most of the other bones were in a fair state of preservation.

As Mrs. Quantrill could not come out on account of the weather, I had the bones put in a small box and put back in the grave, near top, and covered over, and by permission of Mrs. Scally took the skull wrapped in newspaper with me to the hotel to show Mrs. Quantrill. Next morning, I showed it to Mrs. Quantrill, and she was much affected; and she identified a previously described chipped side tooth in lower jaw on the right side. She would not consent to having the skull taken back; as she must have it buried beside his father and brothers in Ohio; and that she would manage in some way to get the other parts of the body.

So the skull was carefully wrapped and put in a basket, and left at hotel check room, while I went back to Samuels Depot, a station several miles south, that she might see Donny Pence, Robert Hall and others of her son's band.

The bones were first deposited in the second-floor room above Scott's newspaper plant at the rear of his home at 308 South Wooster Avenue, Canal Dover. The city fathers refused to allow the remains of the notorious bushwhacker to be buried in Dover's cemetery on East Fourth Street. Several weeks later it was agreed that the remains of Quantrill could be buried there, but only if in a secret and unmarked grave. Only a few people attended the services, among them Caroline Clarke Quantrill and W. W. Scott.

What was buried? No one really knows . . . never will, unless the plot is dug up to determine just how much of Quantrill's remains were actually buried that day early in 1888. As early as December 1887, Scott began writing letters to F. G. Adams, secretary of the Kansas State Historical Society, stating he had positive proof of Quantrill's death, his burial place, and what became of his bones. A letter dated December 17, 1887, written to the society on the official stationery of the *Dover Iron Valley Reporter,* rests proudly among the archives in Topeka. It read:

Dear sir: I have gone on gathering statistics until I have made the complete circle. I was always perfectly convinced as to his (Quantrill) identity, but there were many different stories written as to his origin and early life, that the public was somewhat confused. But I have the written testimony and history from the time he left home in 1857, until he was shot, died and was buried in Kentucky. I have always intended to donate the letters from him, from his comrades, from those who fought him, and from passive citizens who were captured by him, and have so instructed my family, should I drop off suddenly some day.

I have spent much time and money in the collection of this data; and lately made several trips to Kentucky, and had his remains dug up for the satisfaction of his mother, who still lives, and I enclose a lock of his hair, which was buried twenty-two years last June.

I have the indisputable date of when he was shot, when and where he died, and when buried. What would his skull be worth to your society? I am not speculating in dead men's bones, but if I could get a part of the money I have spent, I see no reason why the skull might not just as well be preserved in your cabinet, as to crumble in the ground.

Please consider this letter strictly confidential, and mark your answer "Personal." Destroy this letter when read, and I will do same with yours. No one in the world knows that I can get the head, but I can.

           W. W. Scott

Scott continued to correspond with the Kansas State Historical Society in an effort to sell them the skull of Quantrill, even paying their office a personal visit in 1888, to no avail; the society failed to purchase the gruesome article. It was also in 1888 that Mrs. Quantrill visited friends in Missouri, through the goodness of Scott's heart, for he provided money for her expenses. She became such a nuisance that she wore out her Missouri welcome. Again turning to Scott, she asked for money to return to Canal Dover. Soon after, she had an accident, suffering a fractured arm and shoulder. Scott tried his best to keep her going, but it was a chore. Finally in March 1898, Mrs. Quantrill was admitted to the Home of the Friendless in Lexington, Kentucky.

Soon tiring of the confines of the home, Mrs. Quantrill returned to Canal Dover. There she was placed in the Tuscarawas County Poorhouse until Scott was able to have her accepted in the Odd Fellows Home in Springfield, Ohio. Her husband had been a long-forgotten member of that group, and it was Scott who had uncovered enough data for them to accept Mrs. Quantrill. She died there in 1903 and was buried in the cemetery at Canal Dover, now Dover, Ohio.

W. W. Scott, still endeavoring to sell the skull to the Kansas State Historical Society for a good sum, had given them a shinbone of Quantrill's skeleton. It had been Scott's dream to outlive Mrs. Quantrill so that he could publicize his find and bring himself a small share of fame. However, it was not to be, for he died in 1902, the year prior to Mrs. Quantrill's death.

It is doubtful that Mrs. Scott knew that Quantrill's skull was on the premises at the time of her husband's death. As might be expected in such cases where a family is brought up on historical tales and artifacts, the Scotts failed to appreciate the value of his collection. Most of the Scott collection of Quantrill letters and other papers, as well as the bones of his right arm, were finally purchased by William E. Connelley, who had succeeded F. G. Adams as secretary of the Kansas State Historical Society. These times were most important to Connelley, for he was preparing a book about the noted Quantrill, one that will go down in history as the most remarkable and accurate biography of the Missouri guerrilla.

W. W. Scott's son, Walter, managed to hide the skull long enough to put it to good use. It was used for years in the initiation ceremonies of the Alpha Phi Fraternity, Zeta Chapter. Apparently the Quantrill skull was used in these ceremonies until 1941, when it was purchased by Nelson D. McMillan. It was kept hidden until 1960, when it was brought forth to celebrate the fiftieth anniversary of the Zeta Chapter. After that the skull was again placed in the vault of the McMillan home. There it remained in secret hiding until 1973, when Nelson McMillan, a trustee of the Dover Historical Society, presented it to Sam Ream, historian for the society.

This author visited Dover several times while writing the histories of Quantrill, the Jameses, and the Youngers, only to be met with disappointment and frustration when trying to learn the history Quantrill played in Dover. This city always tried to hide the fact that Quantrill had been born there. Probably this was because Quantrill's brother, B. Franklin Quantrill, had two well-respected daughters, Mary and Nina. Now that those two fine ladies have passed on to their reward, it behooves Dover to take the initiative in the Quantrill matter.

Has Quantrill finally come home?

9.

Ivy Snow: Poison Ivy

This story is true. It was taken from a diary left by Poison Ivy. This diary was last in the hands of her grandson, long deceased, who gave his permission so that this story might be written. Whether the diary still exists is a moot question, but the grandson stated he was going to turn it over to a historical society for the benefit of posterity. It is not known if this ever was done.

Historians inadvisably recorded only those events considered historically significant. They give us but a glimpse of the intimate details of everyday life of the pioneers. Many men and women would have been just as famous as Buffalo Bill or Wild Bill Hickok had anything been written about them. Many of these stories take years of research to verify their accuracy, since details are changed by time and by retelling. Luckily many pioneers kept a diary, otherwise these stories would never be published. Even the diary kept by John Ringo's mother has been the springboard for a book about that famous gunslinger.

Ivy Snow was an infamous character, or perhaps to some extent she was famous. Ivy made Calamity Jane and many other famous or infamous women of the Old West look like Sunday-school teachers. Her family claimed that Ivy was born under a bad sign; they were highly religious people and actually believed this. Perhaps they were right, who knows? But try as they would, they were never able to interest Ivy in church affairs. Ivy was born in Seneca County, Ohio, in 1845; her parents were Walter and Hanna Snow. They were well-to-do farmers by standards of that day. The family never wanted for anything where money was concerned. Ivy's mother said she was a highly intelligent girl and far ahead of her years. When other girls were still playing with dolls, Ivy was looking at men.

One day she informed her mother that she had no intention of marrying one of the local boys. She wanted bigger things from life and someday she would have them. She wanted to be rich and live in a large city.

"I'll never live the drab existence that you have all these years," she told her mother.

Her mother, aghast at such talk, tried in vain to reason with Ivy. This was extremely disheartening to the family; they tried every means, even punishment, to change her attitude, but she remained the same.

At fourteen years of age Ivy had reached full maturity and was considered a beautiful woman. She turned the heads of every male in the community and caused every woman to be jealous. Ivy had no time for local boys; she snubbed them, her head held high. She wanted to give them something to talk about. One boy who decided that he wouldn't be outdone tried to force his attentions on Ivy and nearly went to his grave.

One evening on her way home from the nearby village she was accosted by a young man of the community. She refused to talk to him and warned him to leave her alone. But he had one thing in mind, to sexually attack Ivy. He grabbed her and tried to pull her to him. She jerked out of a razor-sharp knife she carried for just such a purpose and slashed the boy across the midsection. He lay at death's door for weeks, then slowly recovered.

The young man placed the blame on Ivy, as did all the local citizenry. This did not bother Ivy one iota; in fact, she was proud of her accomplishment. It made her famous; people would point her out and say, "There goes that hussy who near stabbed that poor innocent boy to death." This was her first encounter with the authorities but by no means the last. Because of the family prestige the whole matter was dropped; after all, Ivy was only a child. Some people said that Ivy's family would rather she had been raped than bring disgrace to the family as she did.

Unbeknown to her family she was keeping company with an undesirable handsome young man of the community. This man talked Ivy into running away with him. He painted a beautiful picture of the great city and how they soon would be rich. He took her to Boston, where he tried in vain to introduce her into a life of prostitution. She left him and did not return home until she was sixteen years old. How she made her living during those two years is questionable.

When she returned home, her family tried every way to show Ivy the evil of her ways; they were willing to forgive her. She told them in no uncertain words that she was not interested in their sermons. She soon grew tired of her drab home life and made plans to leave.

She called her father and brothers together and told them that she planned to leave the vicinity.

"I'll only bring you more grief and heartache if I stay here," Ivy said. "I want five hundred dollars and a riding horse with a man's saddle."

"You'll not go anywhere!" fumed her father.

"Don't try to stop me, Father. If you do, I'll just leave without any of your precious money."

The father finally gave in. He provided Ivy with the money and the horse, and she was soon on her way to parts unknown.

Near her town John Farmer was getting a wagon train ready to head West. Ivy approached him and told him she wished to buy passage on his train to St. Louis, Missouri. The man laughed at her. The idea of a woman going alone on such a trip was unheard of. Ivy convinced him that she was no ordinary woman. She showed him a knife and a gun and told him she was well able to take care of herself.

"Well," said Farmer, "I need the money and you sure do look like you can take care of yourself, all right."

When the wagon train pulled out, Ivy was there. She wore pantaloons and rode astride her horse like a man. The women of the train were horror-struck, but as Ivy said, "These old biddies don't worry me in the least."

At night she slept in John Farmer's supply wagon. The second night the scout for the party decided to pay Ivy a call. Since she was alone in the wagon, he thought the matter would be an easy one. He forced his way in after Ivy had warned him to keep out.

"What harm can you cause me, you damned vixen?" yelled the man as he lunged for Ivy.

"Just this, you damned fool," cried Ivy as she shot the man in the chest with a derringer. He died instantly.

"Now these old biddies will have something to tell their grandchildren," said Ivy, laughing.

The wagonmaster blamed Ivy for the killing, so when the train reached St. Louis she was turned over to the local police. They had no facilities in the jail for women, so Ivy was placed in a boardinghouse with orders not to leave.

Ivy roamed about St. Louis as she pleased. She rode her horse along the Mississippi River daily. Women looked at her in horror; sitting astride a horse for a woman was strictly indecent. No respectable woman would ride a horse in such a manner. Along the riverbanks she also practiced to shoot her revolver, and she became very proficient with that weapon, as well as being able to throw her razor-sharp knife with deadly accuracy.

Ivy was sure that she would not be convicted for shooting the wagon-train scout, otherwise she would have left town at once, since she had every opportunity to do so. However, she liked St. Louis and wanted to stay there. The War Between the States had commenced and St. Louis was a boom town. There was plenty of money to be made. Although she was only sixteen, Ivy looked more like she was twenty years old. The local authorities, seemingly uninterested in prosecuting Ivy for the murder, decided that the matter should be tried in the locality where the crime was committed. No one ever showed up to press the matter, so Ivy was turned loose. No doubt the authorities had better things to attend to than to prosecute a young woman for defending her honor.

When Ivy accepted a job in a local saloon, one of the better ones in town, she became the center of attraction overnight. Men from all walks of life were struck with her beauty. It did not take Ivy long to work out a second-income matter with two shady characters. Woe to any man who left the saloon with a lot of money and she knew about it. She would pass the word to her accomplices to follow such men from the establishment. They would rob him and split the proceeds with Ivy. Her job at the saloon was to induce men to spend their money. She had no trouble doing this, for men of all ages fell over each other to do her bidding. Ivy worked at this place for nearly a year, all the while piling up a nice bit of money for herself.

At that time the owner of the finest saloon in St. Louis offered Ivy a job. Ivy maintained all through her lifetime that she had never resorted to practicing prostitution, claiming there was a much faster way to make money.

"I always manage to steal money, or work an arrangement with accomplices to do it and we split the take. I always insisted that the victims not be hurt in any way," was the way she responded when asked how she made her money.

When she moved to her new job, Ivy dropped the two men who had been doing her dirty work. She intended to keep to her practice of robbing affluent customers, but she wanted men of a more sophisticated nature to assist her. Her two buddies tried to blackmail her, to no avail.

"You two low-lifers try to mess up my operations at the Palace and I'll cut your throats," she told her two onetime cronies. Apparently they believed her, for they never bothered her again.

Word of Ivy's beauty spread far and wide. As before, men flocked to see Ivy—bankers, buffalo hunters, gamblers, and the like. They all fell in love with her and paid dearly for the privilege. Even Charley Killmer, owner of the Palace, fell to her charms and he asked her to marry him. This was exactly what Ivy had been waiting for.

Once they were married, Killmer thought that he could keep Ivy in their big home. However, the saloon life was too great a beckoning to Ivy, so she stayed in the saloon as she had done so before. Of course, this caused many a heated argument between the two, yet Ivy always got her own way. She even told him that she did not love him and that she had married him only for his money and the saloon.

It was at this time that Ivy was arrested on suspicion of robbery, a charge that was proven against her. Killmer hired the best talent money could buy. It was not long before the smooth-talking lawyers had her free.

One day while riding her charger along the Mississippi she came upon a man in the act of robbing two women. He had forced them to alight from their buggy and was in the act of searching them for their valuables. Ivy was on top of him before he discovered her.

"Drop your gun to the ground," she commanded. To punctuate her demand Ivy fired two shots at the man's feet. The would-be robber lost no time in complying with Ivy's order.

"Now, you filthy scum, I am going to kill you!"

The man begged for mercy, and had not the two women interceded in his behalf, Ivy would have killed him then and there.

"All right, then, into the river with you."

"Lady, I can't swim to the other side, it's too far, more than a mile," the man cried.

"You'll either swim it or I'll kill you right where you stand."

The man threw off his coat and leaped into the river. They watched him as he grabbed on to a floating log and drifted down the Mississippi until he was out of sight. The two women thanked Ivy for what she had done.

"Don't thank me," said Ivy, "but the next time you go out, carry a gun and don't be afraid to use it when necessary."

Ivy's lavish taste for clothes and whatever she wanted caused no end to the fighting between her and Charley. She was tired of him. One day she asked him to take her boat riding on the river.

"It's too dangerous," he told her.

"I live with danger. If you're afraid, I'll go alone."

Several hours later Ivy returned and announced that Charley had fallen into the river and drowned. She told the authorities that she had warned her husband about standing up in the boat, to no avail. Ivy said Charley had stood up in the boat, lost his balance, and toppled overboard.

"I tried to grab him, but the current was too strong and it swept him away," said Ivy.

Everyone suspected Ivy of murdering Charley, but since there were no witnesses, she went free. She now ran the Palace the way she wanted it run. Nothing was barred that would bring in money. She hired the best lawyers to settle the estate of her late husband. In the final outcome she was granted all his assets, including the Palace Saloon.

She operated the Palace until 1864, when she became involved in a cutting scrape. A man had tried to manhandle her, so she cut him several times, to such an extent that he died. By now St. Louis had grown tired of Ivy and her crooked way, so the city fathers ordered her to leave town. It was in St. Louis that she acquired the name of Poison Ivy.

"I'll kill anyone who calls me that!" screamed Ivy. But the name stuck to her for the rest of her life.

She sold all her possessions, except a racehorse, her clothing, and a gold-mounted .32 caliber breech-loading six-gun. She sold out to a millionaire, taking him for plenty, as was her usual custom.

Ivy picked out a reputable wagonmaster who was getting ready to leave for Santa Fe, New Mexico Territory. He gave her a price and told her what she would need. She purchased two covered wagons, three teams of big mules, and hired two drivers named McIntosh and Thomas. The extra team was needed in case something happened to the others. As the train lined up, Ivy's outfit was the finest of the lot. As usual she wore pantaloons and rode her horse astride. As before, the men looked at her with longing in their hearts; the women hated her and were jealous of her beauty and her possessions. She liked to show off by riding her fine horse some distance from the train and then racing back toward it. Ivy usually kept to herself. At night she kept a close watch on her trunks, for in one of those trunks she had a fortune in gold and silver. She cooked her own meals and ate alone. She was not interested in anyone on the train, speaking to her drivers only when necessary.

One night, when they were halfway across Kansas, she stepped from her wagon for a bit of fresh air, when she was grabbed in a bear hug by one of her drivers.

"This is not the time or the place," Ivy told the man.

He turned her loose and stepped back. Ivy quickly drew her knife and stabbed the man. He died shortly thereafter. The killing threw the train into an uproar, and the wagonmaster told Ivy she would have to do her own driving. Naturally, everyone on the train blamed Ivy, never bothering to listen to her side of the story. But Ivy was no ordinary woman. She had the prowess of a mountain lioness when riled, as many folks found out too late. She drove the team of big mules like a mule skinner of long standing, screaming and whistling just to annoy the other women.

When the wagon train arrived in Trinidad, they tried to turn Ivy over to the local authorities.

"We have enough troubles of our own," the local marshal told the wagonmaster. "If you want to try her, do it yourself."

Most everyone believed that the men would be no match for the wily Ivy, so it was decided to allow her to remain with the train. She was also assigned a new driver. He was advised to keep his thoughts to himself and his hands on the reins, or he would probably wind up in an unmarked grave, as Thomas had.

The adults hated Ivy, the children did not. In Trinidad she purchased a bushel basket of candy and passed it among them. From then on, the children called her Miss Ivy.

The train made a short stop at Raton, New Mexico, and then pushed on toward Santa Fe. About two days out of Raton they were hit by a band of Apaches. The Indians were eventually driven off, but the attackers had killed several men and wounded some others. Ivy pitched in and worked like a horse. She helped care for the wounded, washed clothes, and took care of the children. Small as she was, Ivy was a strong woman, and she did not seem to be affected by the illnesses and other problems that befell the other women on the wagon train. After the Indian attack, the folks showed Ivy a little more respect.

Ivy had been warned about riding off from the train, but she rode anyway, not liking to be ordered around by any man. One day she rode off for some distance, and when she turned to ride back to the train, she found herself face to face with six Apaches. Not having seen anything like Ivy before, the braves rode around her, slowly realizing what a prize this would be for their chief. Ivy apprised the situation and then acted. She screamed at her horse and charged the nearest Indian, firing as she went. The Indian was knocked from his horse by her accurate shooting, and Ivy kept riding like the wind. The Indians just sat there and looked, too astonished to move. The men of the wagon train saw what had happened but were too far to offer any kind of assistance to Ivy. At any rate, that day she learned her lesson and she never rode any distance from the train again.

Ivy was not twenty-one years old, and more beautiful than ever. When they reached Santa Fe, Ivy's fame had preceded her. When the train pulled into the big wagon yard, at least a hundred men had turned out to see her. Santa Fe was a wild town with very little law enforcement. President Lincoln had signed the Homestead Act in 1862, and since then thousands of people had migrated West in search of homes to call their own. Some made it, many of them did not. As a writer once said, "Cowards don't come, weak die on the way. Only the strong make it out here, most of them are killed later. It's pure hell for a family. But yet they come." If the number were known who died along the Santa Fe Trail and were buried in unmarked graves, it would be appalling and unbelievable.

Ivy moved her belongings into a hotel and began to look for a place of business. She was satisfied that she could make a go of anything she tried.

There was only one place in Santa Fe she wanted, and it wasn't for sale. It was a fine saloon owned by a man named Joe Horde. Ivy put all the charm that she possessed into this deal. Eventually Joe sold her a half-interest in the place. She drew in the men as she had done in her other places. Most of the dance-hall girls of that day were of the boisterous and awkward type, so Ivy got rid of them and hired girls who were pretty and had femininity. Ivy had been in the business long enough to know what it took to separate a man from his money.

Joe was the jealous type and he did not like the idea of Ivy hanging around other men. When he asked her to marry him, she was quick to accept his proposal. But like her former husband, Horde tried to keep Ivy at home, to keep her happy as a homebody, with a big house and servants. However, again this did not appeal to Ivy, so she spent as much time at the saloon as she had before. One day Joe got into an argument with a gambler over Ivy, and the man shot and killed Joe. Some folks stated that Ivy had set up the whole affair in order to get rid of Joe and collect his wealth. Joe had no immediate family, so there was no haggling over his estate.

So far Ivy had never met a man she really loved. It finally happened, though, with a widower named George Hall, a wealthy rancher who lived outside Santa Fe. He was forty-five years old, but handsome and rugged. In a

short time he fell in love with Ivy and for the first time
in her life Ivy found herself loving someone in return.
There was one problem: Hall had a girlfriend whom he
had been seeing for some time.

This woman called on Ivy and told her to give up on
her idea of marrying Hall. Ivy tried to buy the girl off, to
no avail; she wanted to marry this rich rancher. George
tried his best to find a solution to the problem, but the
girls would have no part of it. One day the two met on
the street and got into a heated argument. A fight en-
sued, and Ivy stabbed this girl to such an extent that
she died three days later. Ivy was arrested and placed in
jail, no bond set. To make matters worse, the girl Ivy
had killed had not been armed at the time of the fight.
People said Ivy must pay for her crime.

Ivy was horror-struck and perhaps a bit frightened for
the first time in her eventful life. She had not wanted to
kill the girl, only to scare her off. She could have hired
someone to kill the woman, had she felt that way about
it. Ivy talked the matter over with George, and they decided that she should escape.

George talked it over with the day jailer. He was
bribed into getting Ivy a pistol. When the night turnkey
came on duty, Ivy pulled the gun on him and in no uncertain terms told him to open the cell or she would
blow out his brains. He believed her. Ivy stepped from
the cell, shoved the jailer into it, and locked the door.
Then she and George mounted their horses and headed
north. Later they were met by George's stepson with two
pack horses. They decided it would not be wise to go to
Raton, so they skirted that town and stopped at Trinidad. From there they headed north and west on a trail
that led to the Spanish Peaks, and then on to a bustling
town named La Veta, which was about fifty miles north
of Trinidad.

La Veta was an ideal spot for their operations. It was
a mining town alive with activity since silver and some
gold had been discovered there, and several coal mines
were also in operation nearby. The mass influx of
miners and others caused them to be able to roam about

unnoticed. However, the inactivity grew on them, so Ivy and George decided to move north, past the Greenhorn Mountains to Pueblo. Soon after they moved west, stopping at Colorado City (now a part of Colorado Springs), and Ivy fell in love with the place. Gold and silver had been found west of Colorado City and also in the south park region and California gulch, and between Pueblo and the Leadville area.

Ivy and George moved farther west, stopping at Tin Cup, where they decided to remain and go into business. They had lumber hauled in from Alamosa and Ivy brought the first piano into that part of Colorado. Ivy opened her saloon and dance hall with a bang, nothing barred. As usual she prospered and men flocked to see this pretty saloon-owner, spending their money lavishly at the gambling tables and for whiskey. Ivy loved this life, especially with George around. But sitting around watching Ivy make up to men became disgusting to George. He longed for his ranch, and although he loved Ivy very much, he could not become accustomed to living in a saloon, so to speak. Ivy refused to accompany him to Santa Fe, fearing the hangman's noose or a long stretch in the state prison.

In a few days George left for Santa Fe, promising Ivy he would keep in touch with her. He also notified the proper authorities that he was coming back to his ranch. When he arrived he was placed under arrest and later tried for his part in Ivy's jailbreak. He was given a suspended sentence and a stiff fine.

It appeared that the authorities were not interested in Ivy's return. They decided to leave her alone as long as she remained outside Santa Fe, or rather New Mexico. They were glad to be rid of her.

Ivy corresponded with George regularly, but steadfastly refused to return to Santa Fe. However, being away from George threw her into a fit of despondency, so she sold out in Tin Cup and moved to Fairplay, where she ran a place for a while, then moved to Georgetown, and then to Dillon, unable to settle down without George's company. Her last attempt at business was in Denver, where she gave up.

"I'm going back to face the music, whatever they do can't be any worse than this misery," she told some friends.

Ivy packed up and headed back for Santa Fe. Even though she had been gone for three years, the authorities were waiting for her when she arrived. She was arrested and released on $10,000 bond. Her first trial ended in a hung jury; the next one was dismissed due to a technicality. The state decided that to try Ivy anymore would be a waste of tax money, so the whole matter was dropped. A Santa Fe lawyer who had been running her saloon in her absence quickly turned it over to Ivy.

She was twenty-eight years old when she finally married George Hall, still the beautiful woman she had always been. She lived at the ranch for a time, keeping to herself, but she had received so much publicity that the population of Santa Fe was not about to let the legend of Poison Ivy die on the vine.

A newspaper reporter dug up everything he could find on Ivy and printed it, always referring to her as Poison Ivy, not Mrs. Hall or anything else, just Poison Ivy. This matter so preyed upon the minds of Ivy and her husband that they decided to take a trip. Perhaps when they returned, people would have forgotten Poison Ivy to some extent.

The Halls left Santa Fe for Denver. From there they went to Kansas City, Missouri, remained there a few days, and then left for New York. Arriving in New York City, they booked passage to England, where they leased a mansion near the ocean. There their first child was born, a boy, and they named him after his father. Three more children were to be born of this union and all four children were reared by a childless sister of Ivy's. Ivy contributed lavishly to their support, giving them everything except a mother's love.

After living in England for two years, the Halls returned to the United States, stopping off in Ohio to pay her folks a visit. However, the longing for the West was strong in their blood, so Ivy and George headed in that direction, leaving their son with Ivy's sister.

Their first stop was Denver. There they found many beautiful hotels and saloons as they made the rounds of the town. Ivy at one time had thought of building a hotel and gambling casino in Denver, but they decided against it. Then another idea came to mind. Why not go to Salt Lake City, Utah? They had heard many nice things about that town and perhaps it might be a good place for them to settle down. So it was agreed they should travel to Utah by wagon so they could get a better idea of what the country was like. They were told that the Indians of the area, the Utes and the Diggers, were friendly and should cause them no problem.

So Ivy and George bought a big covered wagon, two teams of mules, two riding horses, guns, ammunition, cooking utensils, suitable clothing, and food that would not spoil. The trek toward Salt Lake took them through Georgetown, as well as other places that had been stomping grounds for Ivy. However, she made no effort to look up old acquaintances, but forged ahead toward Salt Lake City. Along the way they replenished their supplies as needed, stopping at Glenwood Springs, Colorado, for a few days before venturing across the desert waste.

The going had been extremely rough traveling through the mountains and now it would be desert for some distance. Ivy and George headed northwest, planning to keep this heading until they reached the Utah border. On the third day as they made ready for evening camp, four Indians swooped down upon them and robbed them of everything they possessed. Everything but the gold they carried. Ivy had the habit of hiding the gold in a safe place whenever they camped. The Indians left them nothing, and here they were, stranded in a God-forsaken place, with nothing but a bag of gold.

They spent the night at the intended campsite, heading west and north in the morning. Late that afternoon they reached a creek, more dead than alive from thirst and hunger. There they spent the night.

George hunted along the creek and found some Mexican lemons. These berries are about the size of a small pea and have a sour-sweet taste. They ate some of these and it helped their plight considerably. Having nothing with which to start a fire, George tried rubbing sticks together and managed to have a fire going soon. Since it was cold at night, the fire was a blessing for the two weary travelers. Sometime during the night they heard a call.

"Hey, there, can I come in? I seen yer fire and wanted to make sure you ain't Indians."

"Certainly, please do."

The man approached the camp fire and Ivy and George could see he was riding a horse and also had a pack mule.

"What in tha world happened to you folks, out here alone with no equipment?"

"The Indians raided our camp and took everything we had," Ivy told the man.

"Yep, that's why I was careful in comin' in," said the rider. "I wanted to make plumb certain this warn't a redskin camp. They are plumb bad all around, some of them anyhow. I started to make camp back a ways when I seed yore fire. Shore am glad I did, looks like you all are plumb starved."

With that the man proceeded to unpack his animal and soon had a good meal cooked. It consisted of sow belly and potatoes, and Ivy said she believed it was the best meal she had ever eaten.

The stranger proved to be a prospector from the Blackwater area, a small community some distance away. He told them small quantities of gold had been found in the area, but not enough to start a general stampede of people to the place.

The next morning, with directions given them by the old prospector, Ivy and George headed for Blackwater, a small community which they reached in a few hours. It was located on Black Sulphur Creek about forty miles east of the Utah border. Like many such towns of the Old West, it no longer exists.

After three days in Blackwater, living with a kindly miner's wife, it was decided that George should borrow a horse, ride to Salt Lake City, and buy a new outfit. Ivy wanted revenge and she intended to remain in Blackwater until she had evened the score with the Indians who had robbed them. Since Blackwater was about 150 miles from Salt Lake City, George hired a man to accompany him there. It was a week before George returned.

Ivy and George built a comfortable one-room cabin in Blackwater, then began to check the Indian trading post twelve miles from town. They posed as naturalists studying the area and the ways of the Indians. The Indian agent promised them all the help he could, further advising them that the Indians would cooperate if they were given presents.

They began to cultivate the friendship on an old Indian woman who was at the store every time they visited there. They talked about everything but the raid upon their camp. They also bought her presents of beads, candy, dress goods, and other items she seemed interested in. One day Ivy told her about the robbery. The Indian was silent for a while, then told them that she knew the four young men who had attacked their camp. She was afraid to tell them who the boys were because she feared they would be arrested and put into the white man's jail. Ivy assured her that she only wanted to teach the boys a good lesson.

It was agreed that the Indian woman would tell the boys that two greenhorns were camped at a spring not too far away from the store. The trap was set and they waited. The Indians had nothing to fear from homesteaders, who in general were afraid of Indians. The young Indians rode boldly into Ivy's camp and dismounted. At the same time Ivy and George trained their Winchesters on them. They were ordered to throw down their weapons or die on the spot. They were forced to lie on the ground while Ivy tied their hands and feet with buckskin thongs. She then poured water on the buckskin to keep it tight. The Indians were then dragged behind some nearby rocks and left there. Ivy and George took turns watching the bucks during the night. They pleaded for water but got none. They were going to suffer as had Ivy and George.

No doubt the Indians were dumbfounded. Never had any greenhorns acted like this. Had they known Ivy, they would have stopped wondering. Ivy and George enjoyed a good breakfast while the Indians looked on. They begged for water but got little, just a few drops on their lips. Ivy wanted to keep them alive as long as possible. Sometime during the day all four young Indians were carried into the wagon, and Ivy and George headed the team south.

They continued south for two days, keeping the Indians alive with just enough water to do so, but not giving them a morsel to eat. On the morning of the third day, they arose and made ready to return to Blackwater. Before doing so, however, they cut the Indians loose. They were so weak they could hardly stand. There they left them.

When Ivy and George returned to Blackwater, the Indian agent berated them for their actions. Ivy told him it was none of his damned business what had happened. The old Indian woman, playing both ends to the middle, had told the agent the whole story, but of course did not mention her part in the capture of the four Indian bucks. She also knew that when they returned, if they did, they would never admit to such treatment by a couple of greenhorns.

They gave their shack to the woman who had befriended them when they first arrived in Blackwater, and then left for Salt Lake City. After a stay of six months there, they decided to return to Santa Fe. On doing so, they quickly learned that resentment against them had not died down, so they became disgusted, sold everything they had, and returned to Denver. After a few days there Ivy and George left for Topeka, Kansas. They did not like this place, so they went on to Leavenworth, Kansas, where they learned the Planters Hotel was for sale.

The Planters Hotel had been built in 1858 on the west bank of the Missouri River when Leavenworth was the West's greatest boom town. All ships or riverboats unloaded at the Planters Hotel landing. This hotel was the most magnificent in the West. It was known far and wide and was patronized by those who could afford such luxury. It is known that Jesse and Frank James spent a lot of time at the Planters. This grand old building was razed in 1960, another blot on the pages of progress. It is a shame that it could not have been converted into a museum or put to some similar use.

The available records do not indicate that George Hall purchased the Planters, but Ivy writes in her diary that he did. We know for sure that they did lease it for a number of years.

In 1895 Ivy and George moved to Kansas City, Missouri, where they built a mansion, spending the remaining years of their lives there. Ivy passed away in 1905; George died in 1908.

So ends one of the strangest stories to come out of the Old West.

10.

Belle Starr: Oklahoma Whirlwind

They called her in two ways. One was Cherokee Maiden but the moniker didn't fit. She was no Cherokee and she certainly was no maiden—not by any conception of the word. The other was Queen of the Bandits, a title as fit as any. Spiteful, reckless, headstrong, sort of nice-looking in a rough way, as dangerous as any of the desperados she loved and as lusty as a woman can be, Belle Starr was as romantic and colorful a figure as the West produced.

She married an Indian half her age in full tribal ceremony and was, ironically, a ward of the United States government at the height of her career. In later years she joined forces with Henry Starr, a distant relative of her husband's, who once boasted that he had held up more banks than any other man in history. He was the only man who ever pulled off two bank stickups in the same town on the same day, and he was killed attempting to stick up a bank in the grand old tradition of the frontier—just three years after the close of World War I. In her day, Belle Starr's forest hideout provided safety for some of the most famous outlaws of all times. And yet when legend and rumor are stripped away, hers is probably one of the most vicious of all Western biographies.

Great pains have been taken to check the actual place and birth date of Belle Starr. Many contemporary newspapers claim she was born at Georgia City, Missouri, on February 3, 1846. Members of various bandit families say she was a native of the Kentucky hills. The noted author S. W. Harmon says she was born February 3, 1846, in Carthage, Missouri, while another biographer, Burton Rascoe, is less specific, saying she was born prior to 1848 in Washington County, Missouri.

Although most writers agree with the month and the day, February 3, some have placed her birth as early as 1844. The United States Census records of 1850 and 1860 give the true information. Page 397, R. 518, 1850, clearly states that Myra Shirley was born in 1848, February 5, the date inscribed on her tombstone. The census of 1860, page 827, R. 441, shows her to be twelve years old, clearly establishing the birth year as 1848. It also states that her place of birth was Jasper County and that in 1860 she lived in Marion Township, Carthage, Missouri. She was not actually born in Carthage, but at a point called Medoc, Missouri, ten miles away. The town was later renamed Georgia City. It appears fairly certain, therefore, that she was born in Georgia City, Missouri, on February 5, 1848.

Christened Myra Maybelle Shirley, she later changed her middle name to Belle on a whim of her own. Her father, Judge John Shirley (honorary title) was a farmer and showed real estate at about $600 at the time of Belle's birth. Her father's birthplace is somewhat vague, although census records list the state of Virginia. Little is known about her mother except that she was believed to be Elizabeth Hatfield, related to the feuding Hatfields of West Virginia–Kentucky, and that she went by the name of Eliza. As to the rest of the family there is also conflict. Her favorite brother, undoubtedly Edwin Benton (some said Edward), was eleven years old in

1860, although some say he and Belle were twins. Census records also show Charlotte A. Shirley, twelve years old in 1850, and John Allison Shirley, eight years old in 1850. In 1860 there were two more, Mansfield, eight, and Cravens, age two. The four brothers were born in Missouri and Charlotte was born in Iowa.

In 1860 the Shirleys lived in Carthage, where the judge owned a hotel. He had prospered considerably with real-estate listings of $4,000 and personal property of $6,000. The Carthage Hotel stood on the spot now occupied by the Carter Hardware Company and bore the glaring sign:

CARTHAGE HOTEL
NORTH SIDE PUBLIC SQUARE

John Shirley, Prop.
Horses and Hacks for Hire.
A good stable attached.

Young Belle was educated at the Carthage Female Academy, where she was well liked and considered a very pretty girl. Little is known about her brothers except Edwin, who was called Bud. It was Bud Shirley who probably exerted a stronger influence on Belle Starr than any other person. Bud was still a youngster when he took up arms against the federal troops and was sometimes seen around Quantrill's camp. Some say he was a captain, but he was far too young. Others claim he was also a member of General Jo Shelby's Iron Brigade, but it appears likely that he remained in Missouri hobnobbing with Quantrill or his men except for a brief period when he roamed as a freebooter of so-called southern sympathizers, looting and burning under the guise of patriotism.

Belle early earned her reputation as an expert horsewoman riding to Bud's defense. It was in 1863. Bud was visiting his home in Carthage after serving as a guerrilla for some months, and the federal troops were in constant pursuit. Through the guerrilla grapevine Belle learned that Bud's presence in Carthage was known and Union troopers had been dispatched to arrest him.

Young Belle was in Newtonia, some forty miles away, when she got the news, and she planned to ride to Carthage in order to warn her brother. The federals under direction of Major Eno, however, also had Belle under surveillance and arrested her, keeping her in custody until they were certain she could not reach her brother in time to assist him. They were wrong. On her release, Belle made a wild dash across the rugged countryside, taking to unbroken trails, galloping through creeks and gulleys, and actually outdistanced the Yankee troops. When the soldiers arrived, Bud Shirley had made good his escape.

Some writers have taken great pains to discredit this wild ride, but the concerted efforts of the federal authorities in Missouri to apprehend Belle meant she was giving them a lot of headaches. It is also believed that Belle ran spy letters for Quantrill and this also heckled the federals no end.

A year later in the summer of 1864, young Shirley's luck ran out. He and a companion, Milt Norris, were surprised at the home of Mrs. Stewart near Sarcoxie, Missouri, and Bud was shot to death attempting to make his escape by scaling a fence. Norris escaped and raced to Carthage to tell the Shirley family.

The soldier who killed Bud Shirley was a member of the 15th Missouri Cavalry, Company C, but his name has been lost to the records. A few days later, Belle, only sixteen years old at the time, rode into Sarcoxie with two heavy revolvers strapped around her waist and announced she was there to avenge her brother. No one knows whether she found the Union soldier and had her revenge, but it was generally conceded that the incident was a springboard which launched Belle on her career as a lady bandit.

Rumor had it that Belle, who had ridden into Quantrill's quarters on occasion to deliver messages, now dressed herself like a man and rode with the marauders.

The story seems doubtful since the only record of any woman riding with Quantrill is that of Kate Clarke.

Among the friends of young Shirley was Jim Reed (or Read), the son of a wealthy Missouri farmer. Soon after the death of young Bud, Judge Shirley and his family left Missouri and moved to Dallas, Texas, where the elder Shirley owned a ranch. Shortly after they had moved from the state, Carthage was burned to the ground by federal troops, the Carthage and Shirley house being among those buildings destroyed. It was at the Dallas ranch that Jim Reed courted Belle and finally married her. It has been reported that this marriage was performed while Belle and Reed sat on horseback and that Bloody Bill Anderson, one of the most vicious of Quantrill's raiders, held the bridles, with the aid of John Fisher. Twenty other horsemen witnessed the wedding performed by a justice of the peace. There seems to be some doubt as to the legality of the ceremony, since it is known that the judge and Mrs. Shirley objected to the wedding. Doubts have also been voiced as to the truth of reports on the wedding. It is certain that Anderson played no part since he was killed two years before near Orrick, Ray County, Missouri, and his head was sliced off and stuck on a telegraph pole.

In later years Belle said she married Reed because he had killed the soldier who had slain her brother, and she had vowed to marry the man who avenged Bud's death. At any rate, Judge Shirley did everything in his power to separate the two. Twice they hid her from Reed, and twice he came and took her away. Finally the Shirleys sent Belle to a relative in Colorado. But Reed followed her there and took her back to Missouri with him. The following year, 1869, a girl was born to the couple in Missouri. She was named Rosa Lee Reed and apparently was given to Reed's mother to raise. She was later known to history as Pearl Younger.

It was as Reed's wife that Belle's life of crime really began. Hot-tempered and without conscience after his days with Quantrill, Reed soon was on the run from the law. Jim's younger brother got in a fight at a horse race in Fort Smith, Arkansas, with a man named Fisher. A gunfight followed. The younger Reed was accidentally shot to death by a man named Shannon, who lived on a ranch next to the Reeds. Despite the fact that most people were convinced that the shooting was accidental, Reed sought out Shannon and killed him. Belle and Jim raced across the border into Indian Territory, a refuge for outlaws and killers because they were immune to arrest except by United States government officers.

It was while in hiding that Belle first saw the handsome young Sam Starr, son of Tom Starr, a prominent Cherokee Indian scout who was letting the Reeds use his tepee as a home. Reed was uncomfortable even in the sanctity of the Indian lands, so they left for California shortly, Belle and Pearl making the trip by stagecoach and Jim on horseback. Life in California was good to them. They were happy there, took several trips to Mexico, and in 1871 their second child, a son, was born. They named him Edwin after Belle's slain brother.

It was inevitable that Reed would fall afoul of the law, however, even though this time he was apparently an innocent victim of circumstances. He was arrested for passing counterfeit money, and the officials were about to release him on the charge when they learned he was wanted in Fort Smith for murder.

Reed was out on bond, and when the officers went to rearrest him, they found he had fled their jurisdiction. Reed headed back to the Shirley ranch in Texas while Belle took the long trip around Cape Horn. Jim probably made the journey on horseback, although there is no record concerning this part of the trip. Belle dressed Pearl as a boy so that the authorities would not become suspicious of her. By the time Jim and Belle were together again at the Scyene farm, the judge was reconciled to the marriage, mainly because he had two grandchildren.

In Texas, Belle assumed her role of a shady lady in grand style. She opened a gambling hall in nearby Dallas while Reed remained in the background, helped by people who knew of his southern sympathies during the Civil War and were glad to keep him shielded from the law on the Shannon murder charge. The Younger brothers lived near the Shirley home and Belle was frequently seen in their company. Women of the day whispered about the flashy young Reed woman who paraded down the main street in her daring clothes and dealt faro in the gambling house.

When Jim was arrested on some minor charge by a deputy sheriff named Nichols, Belle openly bragged that she was going to kill the lawman. Shortly afterward Nichols was shot to death in the street. There were no witnesses to the killing, and despite Belle's threats, she was not arrested in connection with the shooting.

Reed was released from jail, since Nichols was the only witness against him on the other charge; the state had no case with their witness dead. Whether Belle actually shot Nichols or not is strictly a matter of conjecture. She was certainly capable of the act and did not stand short on courage. Once when Reed was in jail she went to visit him. Inside the cell they quickly switched clothes, and Reed walked out dressed like a woman. Legally they could have held Belle for aiding and abetting a criminal, but the law was too busy with other matters in the dissension-torn South to bother. She was released without charges being filed against her.

Wanted by the law, Reed turned to his old profession, banditry, riding with a band of gunmen through the territory and adjacent states. But while many accused him of outlawry, others believed that he was a kind of misspent Robin Hood, robbing from the rich and giving to the poor. In 1873 a crime was committed which turned even the most ardent sympathizers against Reed. Jim was recognized as one of the band which went to the home of Watt Grayson, a wealthy Indian, reputed to have a large sum of gold hidden on his premises. Grayson was beaten, then tortured by the thugs, but he refused to divulge the hiding place of the money. The thieves finally turned to his squaw and tortured her until she told them where the gold was. Under the house they found $30,000.

Some reports state that Belle was a member of the band, while others say she was in Dallas at the time. In all fairness to her it must be reported that in 1875 it was learned that the other two men with Reed during the Grayson affair were Dan Evans and Sam Wilder. Evans himself confessed this when he was later arrested for the murder of a cowboy named Seabold of McKinney County, Texas, in 1873. He was hanged for this crime of murder on September 3, 1875, at Fort Smith, Arkansas. Wilder, in the meantime, had already been arrested for another crime and was serving time in the penitentiary when Evans was hanged.

At any rate, the Grayson robbery turned the full wrath of the local people against the Reeds. Belle sprouted out with a full string of racehorses, running them in races throughout Texas, but she was socially ostracized by the people. The long arm of the law, meanwhile, stretched toward Reed. He was killed shortly afterward in what Belle later described as "one of the most treacherous deeds ever perpetrated in the annals of infamy."

Some accounts state that Reed was cut down by Texas Rangers and stated on his deathbed that he had participated in the Gads Hill train robbery in Missouri with Jesse James, and in the Austin–San Antonio stage hold-up. Here is what actually happened:

Soon after the Grayson robbery Reed drifted to Paris, Texas, where he met John Morris. Reed, always willing to help a friend in trouble, loaned Morris $600 after his friend lost all his own money in a high-stakes poker game. Several days later Morris and Reed, riding together, stopped at the home of Charles Lee, fifteen miles from Paris, Texas, where they had breakfast.

Before entering the house, however, Morris suggested they place their pistols in the saddlebags so as not to appear discourteous or suspicious. Reed took off his six-gun and put it in the bag with his friend's weapon. Morris finished his meal first and then walked to the back door, where he suggested to the host that they kill Reed and share the nice reward. The two men shook hands on the deal. Morris went outside, got both guns from the saddlebag, and came back into the house just as Reed was finishing his meal. With both guns cocked, Morris demanded that Reed surrender to his custody.

"Damn you, villain, treacherous coward!" screamed Reed. "I'll die first!"

"Then die!" cried Morris.

Reed leaped to his feet and Morris fired the first shot. The bullet slammed into Reed's chest, but he did not fall. Grabbing a heavy wooden table, he upended it and rushed Morris, using the piece of furniture as a shield. Morris fired several shots through the top of the table, but Reed kept coming. As he approached Morris, the assassin sent another slug splintering through the wood, and Reed toppled over with a bullet in his heart. Although some people reported that Morris sneaked up behind Reed and shot him in the back, Belle and Mrs. Shirley both verified the first report at the time of the shooting. Record shows that Reed died from a bullet fired into his heart from a frontal angle and not through the back.

Morris claimed $1,700 in rewards, but the money did him little good. He was killed shortly thereafter at his ranch near Fort Worth, Texas. The tavern owner received $300 for his minor role in the assassination of Belle Starr's first husband. It is not known whether Belle had anything to do with the death of Morris or not. When she received the news of Reed's murder, she dropped to her knees and, overcome with grief, swore in the presence of God to avenge the death of her husband. Those who knew Belle later stated that her grief was due more to rage than to actual sorrow. At any rate, she berated the remainder of the Reed family for not taking up arms against Morris. There were rumors at the time that she even refused to identify the body of her husband to keep Morris from receiving the reward, although it is doubtful she ever saw the body and it seems certain now that Morris did get his blood money.

Belle's reputation had suffered immensely during her flamboyant Dallas days and the rampages of Jim Reed before he was killed. It became manifest in the fact that even old Judge Shirley, a once-respected member of the community, paid for her wickedness. Belle returned to her father's farm in Scyene soon after Reed's death and found the family virtually blacklisted by the entire community. In 1876 Judge Shirley died and was buried in an unmarked grave in a nearby cemetery. Efforts to locate the grave have been fruitless. Belle's mother, heartbroken at the death of her husband and the contempt suffered by the family because of her daughter's exploits, moved back to Missouri.

In 1876 Belle opened a livery stable on the outskirts of Dallas, and rumors began to spread that local outlaws were seen there frequently. The stable soon was suspected as a storeplace for stolen horses, with Belle acting as a fence for the animals. The James brothers and the Youngers among them stopped off at Belle's place at times. People began to speak of Belle in whispers behind their hands, saying that she frequently visited the homes of strange men for other than livery-stable business. She once acquired $2,500 in one lump sum from a wealthy cattleman named Patterson. Why she got it is anyone's guess, but she used the money to send her two children to school at Rich Hill, Missouri, the home of Reed's mother.

In 1878 Belle was finally arrested for having stolen horses in her possession. In no time she landed in a Dallas jail. Never one to stand long on ceremony, Belle flirted with a deputy and soon had him eating out of her hand. He helped her to escape and even accompanied her, but he was back in a few days, tied to his horse with a note pinned under his badge, "Returned for unsatisfactory reasons." Yes, that was like Belle, all right.

Belle's list of lovers was long and impressive. She even circulated the rumor that she was one time married to Cole Younger, the noted Missouri outlaw. These reports were further bolstered by the fact that Pearl Reed sometimes went under the name of Pearl Younger. Others said she was married to Bruce Younger, a rough and rugged miner who lived at Galena, Kansas, a tough mining camp of that day across from Joplin, Missouri. Some writers say Bruce was Cole Younger's brother, others that he was a cousin. Records show that Bruce Younger actually was a half-brother to Cole's father, and was the black sheep of that family. Living relatives of Cole confirm these findings. Later Bruce Younger married an Indian girl, but there is no record of any betrothal to Belle.

Investigation also produces another Bruce Younger, age eighteen, in 1850, the son of Coleman Younger, Liberty Township, Clay County, Missouri, who was forty years old at that time. This Bruce, in fact, was a cousin of the bandit Cole Younger, but his name Bruce is preceded by the initial C. There is no record of this Bruce having wed Belle. There is, of course, plenty of reason to believe that Belle perhaps did have an affair with one of these men. It was not uncommon in those days for a woman to claim to be a man's wife without going through the bothersome formality of a ceremony.

Another on Belle's list was a man named Blue Duck. He was an Indian outlaw leader. Belle was queen of this gang for a while. We have no other record of this outlaw's name other than Blue Duck, which is the English translation of his Indian name.

The gang rustled cattle, horses, and raided small banks and held up stages in the Indian Territory. Belle was a fiery and demanding figure of royalty in this desperado empire. Once while riding on the prairie, Belle's hat flew off. When Blue Duck made no effort to retrieve it, Belle drew her revolver and promptly demanded a little respect. Her lover quickly fulfilled her wish, got her hat, and they continued on their ride. But if she was harsh in her demands for courtesy, Belle was just as efficient when it came to playing her part in the gang. Blue Duck on one occasion dipped into the outlaw brood's treasury and skipped into Dodge City, Kansas, with $2,-000 for a little gambling. He dropped the whole bundle. The next night Belle appeared at the gambling hall, gun in each hand, and lifted the entire bankroll of the house. She made quite a profit. Her take was $7,000. On the way out she informed the aghast owner that she didn't have time to count the loot, but if she got more than Blue Duck had lost, he could bounce on over into Indian Territory and collect the change. There is no record of the owner bouncing over.

Her affections for Blue Duck seemed genuine. On June 23, 1884, her lover was arrested for the murder of a young man named Wyrick. Suspected of the murderous deed were Blue Duck, William Christie, and Martin Hopper, the latter a relative of Blue Duck, on whose farm the Wyrick boy had been killed. Immediately following the murder, Blue Duck disappeared, but Hopper was arrested and brought in for questioning. However, the authorities were unable to hold Hopper due to insufficient evidence.

Shortly after, William Christie was arrested on a charge of peddling whiskey in the territory. The authorities did not wish to alert Blue Duck by charging Christie with the murder of Wyrick, so they made their prisoner a proposition. If Christie would lead the lawmen to Blue Duck's hideout, they would drop the whiskey-peddling charges against him. Eager to jump at such a chance, the perfidious Christie led the officers to the hideout. There Blue Duck was promptly arrested and he and Christie were taken to Fort Smith, where Blue Duck was questioned.

During the course of the investigation, circumstances were brought to light which implicated William Christie in the murder of Wyrick, and he was held over for the grand jury. That body, however, failed to indict him, so he was permitted to return home.

Failing to keep their promise to Christie about the whiskey-peddling charge, he was arrested by the officers, brought to court, and sentenced to the county jail for a year. While serving his term, Christie was again investigated by the grand jury, indicted, and held on a murder charge, along with Blue Duck.

At the trial the first man to take the stand was William Christie. He testified that on the day Wyrick was slain he and Blue Duck were at the home of a man named Ross, some three miles from the Hopper residence, and that all of them were drunk. He further stated that after leaving the Ross home he and Blue Duck went to visit Hopper, but found him not at home, so they decided to wait for him. Christie claimed that when Mrs. Hopper went to the spring for a bucket of water, he rested on the porch, dozed off, and did not awaken until he heard five pistol shots fired in rapid succession. He also stated that he was alone and that when he sat up he saw Wyrick's plow horse coming dashing into the yard, and that he caught the animal and tied it to the fence. Christie further claimed that at the time Blue Duck approached he was carrying Martin Hopper's revolver in his hand and that the gun was empty.

When placed on the witness stand Mrs. Hopper repudiated Christie's statement, stating that when she appeared shortly following the shots, Christie was holding the pistol and not Blue Duck; also that he took six cartridges from a cartridge belt and gave them to Blue Duck, telling him to reload the weapon. At that time Blue Duck mounted his horse and left.

Hawky Wolf testified that Blue Duck came to his home and fired a shot at his son, Willie Wolf, and three shots at himself, all of the bullets missing; also that Blue Duck had told him he had just killed Wyrick over at Hopper's place. Evidence also was brought out that neither Blue Duck nor Willie Christie was armed at the Ross place. If neither man was armed at the Ross house, how did Blue Duck come into possession of Martin Hopper's pistol, and where did Christie obtain the full belt of cartridges for the weapon, unless Hopper had a hand in the crime?

Blue Duck denied all the evidence submitted. Martin Hopper dodged the law and was not present during the proceedings. Hanging Judge Parker's court found Blue Duck guilty, but William Christie was acquitted.

Blue Duck didn't have a chance in Parker's court and neither did any other criminals brought before that bench. On August 10, 1873, President U. S. Grant appointed Judge Parker federal judge for the District Courts for the Western District of Arkansas with criminal jurisdiction over the Indian Territory, and he really took his work seriously. In the more than twenty years he served before dying in office November 17, 1896, Hanging Judge Isaac Parker disposed of no less than eighty-eight men on his gallows. Needless to say, Blue Duck got the limit. Tried in 1885, Blue Duck was convicted on January 30, 1886, and sentenced on April 30, the date of his execution set as July 23, 1886.

No one gave Blue Duck much of a chance after that, since anyone given such a sentence in the court of Judge Parker seldom did not hang. But Belle Starr did not rest a minute. She engaged the legal services of the famous J. Warren Reed and raised enough money to take the case out of Judge Parker's hands. They went directly to the President of the United States, and finally were able to have Blue Duck's sentence commuted to life imprisonment.

"There's no prison in Arkansas that will hold that Indian," were the words on everyone's lips, so Blue Duck was taken to the Southern Illinois penitentiary at Menard. The records there say that he was not married. There he remained a prisoner until March 20, 1895, when he was pardoned and left the prison a free man. It was not long after that he became involved in a fatal disagreement in a Kansas gambling house and ended up in the local cemetery.

After Blue Duck had been lodged in the Menard prison, Belle sped back to Indian Territory, to the home of her husband, Sam Starr, son of Tom Starr, whom she had married on June 5, 1880, according to the official records of the Canadian County, Cherokee Nations, marriage records. There it says in Vol. 1 B, page 297: "Marriage report. On the 5th day of June, 1880, by Abe Woodall, District Judge for Canadian District, Cherokee Nation, Samuel Starr, a citizen of the Cherokee Nation, age 23 years, and Mrs. Belle Reed (Reid), a citizen of the United States, age 27 years.

H. J. Vann, Clerk"

It appears that Sam Starr gave his correct age, but we know for certain that Belle was much older than twenty-seven years. Strangely enough, when Sam took Belle as his wife, the U.S. government, by law, took her as a ward, so the bandit lady actually was now the government's full responsibility.

This seemingly had little effect on her conduct or on Sam's. With her handsome Indian husband Belle took up a thousand-acre claim on the Canadian River near Eufaula, Oklahoma, and moved into a log cabin that was standing there. They named the location Younger's Bend, a somewhat romantic name for the new bride to pick, considering her past experiences with some of the Youngers. Many claimed she did name the area after Cole Younger. Even today there is a school there bearing the name of Younger's Bend School. Belle decorated the walls of the dim little abode with colored linen she purchased on frequent trips to St. Louis. Belle also became quite the fashion plate in this period of her life. She took up the sidesaddle, apparently because it was the accepted way for a lady to ride in Europe, and she created quite a figure dashing about on a specially made saddle which appropriately was called the Starr saddle.

Younger's Bend became a popular meeting place for some of the most notorious outlaws of the day. The low-slung, tiny cabin witnessed many outlaw revels which included the appearance of members of the Jesse James gang. A popular rumor that the bandits hid their loot near the cabin created a furor in later years, and people flocked to the scene with shovels, virtually plowing up the whole area in search for the ill-gotten riches. None of it was ever found. The robbers of the day did not bury their loot like the old-time sea pirates, they simply spent it as fast as they stole it. Stories even circulated that Cole Younger once made a stop at the house after a man said he saw an outlaw around the place wearing those famous handmade leather boots with C.Y. branded into them. The story is false. The boots with those initials might have been seen, but Cole Younger certainly was not wearing them. Cole was arrested in 1876 and was in prison years before Belle ever moved to the Bend.

Rumors of the happy and unlawful days at Younger's Bend eventually reached the ears of Judge Parker, and the Hanging Judge sent a posse of deputies out to arrest the whole lot. A friend of the Starrs was waiting when the lawmen arrived, telling the group that the former occupants had moved away. The deputies left without a search; Belle and Pearl, who were hiding inside, returned to their chores.

Parker was not to be denied, however. Shortly after their first visit to Younger's Bend, officers of Parker's court paid a second visit, this time arresting Sam and Belle on a charge of horse theft and possession of liquor, a federal offense in the Indian Nations. The Starrs claimed they were framed and Parker apparently believed them. They were given relatively light sentences of one year each in the Detroit, Michigan, House of Correction.

There has been varied opinion on what happened to Pearl Reed during her mother's incarceration at Detroit. Some say she lived with a family named McLaughlin in Parsons, Kansas, and others say she lived in Oswego. In a letter from Belle to Pearl, reference is made to Mamma Mac, which might well be Mrs. McLaughlin. The letter was sent to Oswego, Kansas, and was first published by the noted Western authority Harmon in 1899. He claimed it was genuine and it appears to be. It seems a well-written letter for Belle to compose, but she did have a fair education, and then, too, the original letter might have been edited by someone else along the line.

My Dear Little One:
It is useless to attempt to conceal my trouble from you and though you are nothing but a child I have confidence that my darling will bear with fortitude what I now write.

I shall be away from you a few months, baby, and have only this consolation to offer you, that never again will I be placed in such humiliating circumstances and that in the future your tender little heart shall never ache again, or a blush called to your cheek on your mother's account. Sam and I were tried here, Jim West, the main witness against us. We were found guilty and sentenced to nine months at the House of Correction, Detroit, Michigan, for which place we start in the morning.

Now Pearl, there is a vast difference in that place and a penitentiary; you must bear in mind, and do not think of mama being shut up in a gloomy prison. It is said to be one of the finest institutions in the United States, surrounded by beautiful gardens with fountains and everything nice. There I can have my education renewed, and I stand sadly in need of it. Sam will have to attend school and I think it is the best thing that ever happened for him, and you must not be unhappy and brood over our absence. It won't take long for the time to glide by and as we come home we will get you and then we will have such a nice time.

We will get your horse and I will break him in, and you can ride John while I am getting Loco. We will have Eddie with us, and will be gay and happy as the birds we claim at home. Now baby, you can either stay with grandma or Mamma Mac, just as you like and do the best you can until I come back, which won't be long. Tell Eddie that he can go down home with us and have a good time hunting, and though I wish not to deprive Marion and Ma of him any length of time, yet I must keep him a while. Love to Ma and Marion.

Uncle Tom has stood by me nobly in our trouble, done everything that he could do. Now baby, I will write you often. You must write to your grandma and don't tell her of this; and your Aunt Ellen, Mamma Mac, but to no one else. Remember, I don't care who writes to you, you must not answer. I say this because I do not want you to correspond with anybody in the

Indian Territory. My baby, my sweetheart, my little one, and you must mind me. Except Auntie—if wish to hear from me, Auntie will let you know. If you should write me, Ma would find out where I am and Pearl, you must never let her know. Her head is over-burdened with care now, and therefore you must keep this carefully guarded from her.

Destroy this letter as soon as read. As I told you before, if you wish to stay a while with your Mamma Mac, I am willing. But you must devote your time to your studies. Bye, bye, sweet baby mine.

Belle Starr

There has been some question as to the authenticity of this letter since it should be noted that the letter was not signed mother, which would have been proper in this case. It is also seen that Belle referred to her sentence as nine months when actually she got a year. This letter was supposedly written to Pearl in February 1883, shortly before Belle left for Detroit. How did she know she was going to serve only nine months before she was paroled? Besides, why was the letter not destroyed?

On the other side of the ledger there are folks who claim they saw Belle write and mail the letter at Fort Smith. It was addressed to Pearl at Oswego, Kansas. A member of the Robinson family at Joplin, Missouri, stated he saw Pearl Reed living at a hotel in Parsons, Kansas, in 1882 or 1883, and that the hotel was operated by a family named McLaughlin.

On release, the Starrs returned to Younger's Bend with Pearl and Mabel Harrison, an orphan Belle brought with her from Missouri. The two girls attended school at Briartown, and for a while things at the Bend seemed quiet and happy. Sam, however, had already had his taste for quick riches, and the law was soon on him again, this time for a post-office robbery. He fled to New Mexico. A short time later Belle was under indictment for stealing horses again. She certainly did not live up to her promise to Pearl about going straight. The following item appeared September 20, 1886, in the *Little Rock Gazette:*

Ft. Smith, Sept. 18—Belle Starr, who is here on bond awaiting trial, has received word from her home on the Canadian River stating that her husband, Sam Starr, who had been dodging officers for several years, had been badly wounded in a conflict with the Indian police. Belle said her information was that police fired on and wounded Sam, killing his horse, without demanding his surrender and that fifty shots had been exchanged in the fight. Belle has the court's permission to be absent until next Wednesday, and will leave in the morning for her husband's bedside.

Apparently Sam's wounds were not as bad as the item intimated. He regained consciousness in the sheriff's office where he had been taken after the shooting, seized a guard's gun, and escaped. When Belle returned to Younger's Bend she found him hiding in the brush. It appeared that Belle was beginning to tire of running. She advised her husband to surrender, and he returned to face the court.

Sam Starr was arraigned and trial was set for March 7, 1887. He was released on bond and with his wife, Pearl, and Mabel started for the Bend to await the court proceedings. En route they stopped at the home of Lucy Surratt to relax. A dance was in progress and one of those present was Frank West, one of the possemen who had fired on Sam. Witnesses stated that as Sam entered the room and saw West he drew and fired without warning. Mortally wounded, West fell to the floor but managed to pull his gun and fire back. When the smoke cleared, Belle Starr was again a widow.

The charges against Belle were dropped after the death of Sam Starr, and once again she returned to Younger's Bend. For several months after her husband's death, Belle threw in her lot with Henry Starr, a relative of her late husband, who carried out a series of small raids and bank robberies in the territory and adjacent states. There were rumors that Belle became a coleader of the Starr gang, but these never were founded. Starr was probably the last of the great frontier bank robbers. His association with Belle, however, was short.

Belle soon began to appear at carnivals, state fairs, and in theaters, making a living as one of the leading attractions of the day. Her daring exhibitions of marksmanship and riding attracted crowds from miles around, and she frequently took part in a sham stagecoach holdup in which the boisterous Hanging Judge Parker played the role of a passenger.

In 1887 Belle learned that Pearl was pregnant. Although Pearl told her mother she had married a half-breed Cherokee boy in 1886 in a ceremony prescribed by white laws, Belle had the young Indian run out of the territory. There is evidence that Pearl fled to the home of the Reeds in Rich Hill and had her baby. However, by using forged letters and trickery, Belle brought Pearl back to the Bend and had the child admitted to an orphanage. At any rate, Pearl never saw her baby again. It was the general opinion that Belle seriously mistreated her daughter, virtually keeping her a prisoner at Younger's Bend.

In 1887 Pearl married a Cherokee Indian named Nilly or Jim July, but the vicious-tempered Belle refused him admittance until he changed his name to Starr. Edwin Reed also had turned bad and was considered a troublemaker and a bully. In her attempts to straighten the youth out, Belle often bullwhipped him mercilessly. The boy openly hated his mother, even threatening at times to kill her. It appeared that Belle, embittered after her long years on the wrong side of the law and the loss of two husbands and several lovers, was now trying to regain some semblance of respectability. Her efforts were to little avail, however. Jim July was a horse thief, and was later shot to death by U.S. Deputy Marshal Bud Trainer in Choctaw County. Edwin was killed while shooting up a saloon in Wagoner in 1896.

In the late eighties a man named Edgar Watson moved onto a farm on the south side of the Canadian River about seven miles from Younger's Bend. Watson appeared to be a law-abiding man, and merchants with whom he dealt expressed the utmost faith in his integrity and honesty. Belle had wormed her way into Watson's confidence, however, and learned that he was suspected of murder and wanted in Florida.

The *Kansas City Star* on April 10, 1910, in an item on Belle Starr, gives a description of Belle's murder. The paper also intimates that Watson and July were engaged in stealing horses, and Watson had refused to make a fair division of the spoils. Belle then threatened to betray him.

On Sunday, February 3, 1889, Belle rode into the King Ranch store and gin, and told the proprietor she had come to eat dinner with him. The previous day Belle had accompanied July partway to Fort Smith, where he was going to answer a horse-theft charge. She was riding her favorite mare, a fast, spirited animal. At dinner she appeared worried and apprehensive, and told the guests that she had a premonition of death. She was laughed at and the comment was made, "Thunder and lightning couldn't kill you."

Before she left the ranch Belle snipped a large silk handkerchief in half, gave half of it to a tenant farmer's wife as a keepsake, and left a cloak for which she paid forty dollars with the store proprietor for safekeeping.

Belle left the store at 1:00 P.M., and before reaching the river stopped at the home of a man named Barnes, where she passed the time talking with the women until about 3:00 P.M. When she arrived there, Watson was standing in the backyard with a shotgun. He left at once in the direction Belle would travel. Belle left after getting some corn pone from Mrs. Barnes. At 4:00 P.M. Mike (Frog) Hoyt, a farmer, was crossing the river on a ferry when he heard a rapidly running horse coming through the underbrush. He saw Belle's riderless mare leap from the embankment into the river and swim

across. Hoyt rode back up the road. At a sudden turn in
the trail his horse pulled up short and snorted. The
body of Belle Starr lay in the middle of the wooded
trail.

Belle was killed with two loads of mixed shot from a
shotgun. She apparently had been shot in the back and
had fallen into the road with her face in the mud.
While lying there unconscious, her assassin walked up
beside her, took her own revolver from its holster, and
shot her in the head. The weapon was then replaced.

Most of the local residents believed that Watson was
the killer. Tracks led from the scene to a point near his
home. There were also those who thought that perhaps
Ed or Pearl had exacted their toll of vengeance for the
mean way in which Belle had treated them and that one
of them had been responsible for her death. Watson was
arrested, but was released on lack of evidence. Later he
found his way back to the Island of Chokoloskee in the
Florida Everglades where they meet the Gulf of Mexico.
This island was used by outlaws and deserters during
the Civil War, and for the most part was seldom visited
by anyone. Watson proclaimed himself "emperor" of the
island and ruled for a number of years. On October 24,
1910, a handful of honest fishermen shot and killed Watson on the boat landing at the store of Ted Smallwood.
He was first buried at Rabbit Key and later reburied in
the Fort Myers cemetery. So passed the man of whom it
was said: "He killed the famous Belle Starr."

Belle was dressed for burial by the women in the
neighborhood. Her grave was dug in the dooryard and
she was buried without a prayer, a pistol in her right
hand. Some sensationalists have claimed that this
revolver was once the property of Cole Younger. Her
grave was marked by a rough stone wall two feet high,
with two large slabs tilted over the top in a V shape.
The stone was carved by Joseph Dailey, a local stonecut-
ter, whose name appeared in the lower left-hand corner
of the original stone. The grave is on the Belle Starr
Ranch (Younger's Bend), thirteen miles from Eufaula,
Oklahoma. The tombstone, ironically, was paid for by

Pearl Reed with money earned in the Pea Green Bawdy House at Fort Smith.

The original headstone was inscribed:

BELLE STARR
Born in Carthage, Mo.
Feb. 5, 1848
DIED
Feb. 3, 1889
Shed not for her the bitter tear
Nor give the heart a vain regret,
'Tis but the casket that lies here,
The gems that filled it sparkles yet.

Belle's daughter, Pearl Reed, died in Douglas, Arizona, on July 8, 1925, and was buried in Calvary Cemetery in that city.

At the time this author visited that area it was almost impossible to locate the exact spot of Belle's grave, and it was accessible only by foot or by jeep. We do know that one day someone opened the grave and removed the pistol that had been placed in Belle's dead hand.

Strange as it may seem, no one in Eufaula had ever seen the grave of Belle Starr. At Porum, Oklahoma, on the Canadian River, it was learned that Claude Hamilton had taken over the grave property and some surrounding acreage in a back-tax sale. It is such a desolate and forlorn spot that none ever visit it. Mr. Hamilton, seeing that roaming cattle had broken some of the grave marker stones, rescued them and placed them in a safe place, keeping them for another day's use. Perhaps one day a stream of tourists will pass the spot and gaze in wonderment at the grave of Belle Starr, just as they now do at the grave of Missouri's Jesse James and at the last resting place of other famous frontier characters.

The few people who do know the grave's exact location are keeping silent about it. At least when this author was there, no one gave any idea as to exactly where the grave was. Thus the remains of the once-colorful Belle Starr, a woman who loved attention and notice, lies in an unmarked grave, gone but not forgotten, the general area of the grave now covered with stone slabs and surrounded by a wire fence and overrun with weeds and poison ivy.

11.

◆━◆

Florence Quick: Lady of Shifting Names

Oklahoma lawmen cursed and joked about her. Not even the late Belle Starr could have outdone her in wit, daring, and cunning. She earned all those many monikers she wore while riding as "spotter" for one of the most notorious wild bunches in all Western history. Florence Quick was her baptismal name, but was worn less often than all of her several aliases. However, she never attained by wedding ceremony the name she most wanted to bear. . . .

Florence was a tall, graceful Missouri girl who went bad. For money, advantage, or wanting to help her friends of the thieving Dalton bunch, she slept with a lot of men while remaining, in her deepest feelings, loyal to Bob, the leader.

She was born shortly after the Civil War—possibly in 1867—near Belton, Missouri, a small town south of the Kansas border. Her father, a sharp trader, was a wily cattleman who had been married three times and had piled up a lot of money while successfully avoiding fighting for either North or South during the showdown over slavery.

"During her childhood years Florence was a perfect little lady, thoroughly feminine, pretty, brunette, not at all tomboyish," so her second cousin, Keene Wallis, would describe her from family memories in a letter to Dalton gang historian Harold Preece dated July 1, 1962.

"She could ride a horse," Mr. Wallis added, "and she could shoot—but who except me in the family couldn't." This informant, a distinguished American poet, also added that his mother, her first cousin, had also been Florence's schoolteacher.

Not many miles from the Quicks lived a family of mixed reputation: the Daltons. The father of this huge clan, Lewis Dalton, was a Kentucky-born wanderer who, like Dan Quick, had managed to evade military service during the Civil War. But he did not have Dan's acumen about making a buck and keeping it.

Lew was a wandering fiddler, carnival roustabout, and hanger-on at racetracks. He came home just often enough to give his long-suffering wife, a relative of the outlaw Younger boys, "fifteen successive children."

Nine of these were sons. Five would become men of the gun. They were Frank, an Indian Territory marshal dying honorably in line of duty; Bill, who for a time would be a minor political figure in California but who died an outlaw in Oklahoma; Emmett, a cocky show-off surviving citizens' bullets in Kansas; Bob, chief of the pack, a devil with women, who died, like Grat, in Coffeyville, where everybody remembered the Dalton family as "sometimes charity cases."

Whether Florence Quick knew Bob Dalton back there in Cass County, Missouri, seems uncertain. But the possibilities are that they recognized each other by sight at least. For country people of that time had nodding acquaintances with many other folk they met, maybe at revival meetings, in general stores, or at livestock auctions.

But the ladylike little girl grew aggressively direct in her behavior toward males when she reached that dangerous age of fourteen. So her parents sent her to a strictly run school at Nolden, Missouri. Later, it is said, the Quick family moved temporarily to Indian Territory. There also, the Daltons would migrate, settling near Vinita in the Cherokee Nation.

Florence allegedly got into trouble—that nineteenth-century euphemism for seduction—at the strict school. So she was reportedly booted out during her first and only semester. She too went to Indian Territory. Rapidly she became a top-notch whore as well as a promising apprentice in general outlawry.

Her main instructor was an Indian woman named Jessie White Wings, who could assertedly outgamble any white man in the territory. As Jessie's protégée, Florence learned gambling and whoring. During a period when the Indian republics were dying from the increasing white overflow, this white woman assumed her first alias: a male moniker, Tom King. She also acquired the territory's most common and lucrative form of thievery: horse stealing.

It is not known from what gang of bronc snatchers she picked up the trade, but she learned all that there was to know about it: how to scout a horse range with the least risk of detection and how to lead male cohorts to it afterward; how to snip a pasture fence quickly and deftly with wire cutters; how to alter brands after the ponies had been driven to some temporary hideout pending sale to buyers of hot stock; how to palaver the best prices for the merchandise; how to get out of jail if arrested . . . and in that art Tom King was a genius.

Often her deft fingers manipulated dexterously the locks of flimsy jails. At other times, it is probable, she did business with her captors, exchanging love for liberty. No bars held this agile country girl. No court ever convicted her. In Indian Territory and part of a chunk that later became Oklahoma, it was hard to get a verdict against anybody for stealing horses or cattle—maybe because so many outwardly respectable citizens were involved, directly or indirectly, in the traffic.

Few women were ever brazen enough to put on male attire in the Old West—not even the painted saloon and dance-hall charmers. Flo, alias Tom, wore pants and men's shirts whenever necessary for her business. Skirts would have been a hindrance in horse stealing.

How this lady long rider happened to adopt the alias of Tom King also seems uncertain. Maybe because it was short and pithy, easily remembered. Her cousin, Keene Wallis, suggested that she may have borrowed it from one of her transient paramours.

Did her preference for male garb also imply lesbian tendencies? Who can say? Few people back then even knew that sexual deviates existed.

Did Miss Quick meet other émigrés—the Daltons—in Indian Territory and spot them as one-time Missouri neighbors? Harold Preece thinks it very possible that she did. He feels that there could have been sociable re-unions at country parties or chance meetings on rural roads. However, love did not wrap itself right soon around this destined pair—Florence and Bob.

Bob Dalton was "that way" about his first cousin, Minnie Johnson, sometimes known as Minnie Dalton, because she lived with the Daltons at Coffeyville. During 1886, the shabby clan had made one more move to that Kansas community, which held them in no large esteem. Adeline (Ma) Dalton had divorced profligate Lewis, who had moved to nearby Dearing. The rowdy boys had become apprentice lawmen in Indian Territory, earning two dollars per arrest plus whatever they could graft on the side.

It is not on record that either of the boys ever put the cuffs on that lawless young lady from back home— Florence Quick.

During 1887 Deputy Marshal Frank Dalton was shot down in Arkansas River bottoms by a young bootlegger named Bill Towerly. Grat, his posseman or aide, was promoted to the deputy's job left vacant by the slaying of his brother. Bob, then seventeen years old, took Grat's former post. Sixteen-year-old Emmett Dalton, who would grow up to concoct so much fable about Florence Quick and the deadly Dalton gang, left off cowpunching to collect what he could by riding around wearing a star with his cash-hungry brothers.

On a family visit to Coffeyville, Bob and Emmett found that Bob's time with luscious cousin Minnie had "been beat" by a hired hand and alleged ex-bootlegger, Charley Montgomery. Minnie gave Bob only a cousinly peck on the cheek. She made it pretty plain that there would be no more love-ins between the two.

By the Dalton logic, there was only one way of eliminating a rival: kill him, which these two Daltons—Bob and Emmett—set out to do after Minnie and Charley had eloped. As soon as Minnie was discovered missing from the house, the two brothers rode off, hoping to intercept them at the railroad station where hopefully Charley would be executed by the pair and Minnie brought back for a sound thrashing with a cartridge belt—sometimes a punishment for faithless women in the Old West. But Bob did shoot into the train, missing those two as it whizzed by. From the window Charley Montgomery raised a mocking head.

Fifteen-year-old Minnie allegedly died a prostitute in a red-light section of Kansas City. In not too long a time she would be replaced by that scarlet widelooper, Florence Quick, as the mate of Robert Renick Dalton. However, Charley Montgomery did get killed by the avenging brothers . . . finally.

They shot him dead at the ranch where he had worked and was returning to pick up his effects. Then they carried his corpse to a town undertaker, not wanting to mess with Daltons. "Bury him," Bob ordered curtly. "He was resisting arrest. Charge it to the government."

At age eighteen, by federal-court appointment, Bob Dalton became police chief of the Osage Nation. His main assignment from the U.S. district judge in Wichita, Kansas, was to root out bootleggers infesting this stretch of Indian Territory; brother Emmett became his posseman. But the teenage law enforcer soon became the largest purveyor of illicit whiskey in the crime-infested Osage Hills. There, it is said, he and Florence Quick got together though some place their rawhide romance as starting in Tulsey Town, an Indian community destined to become the city of Tulsa.

From some previous dealings of her own, Flo knew every whiskey still and every whiskey maker in the Osage Nation. She collected protection money from the distillers: cash shared with Police Chief Dalton, some going also to posseman Emmett. He had an acquisitive little girlfriend, Julia Johnson (no kin to Minnie), who lived near Bartlesville.

Came the great land runs of 1889 with the western part of Indian Territory being ripped off for white settlers and named Oklahoma Territory. Its capital was the mushrooming town of Guthrie, with the redoubtable Bat Masterson once having been there to establish law and order. Florence Quick was often seen on its teeming streets.

Bob, Grat, and Emmett Dalton, licensed officers of the law, took up another profitable sideline—horse stealing, with Florence Quick, it is said, helping to locate likely remudas for sale at the equine black market in Baxter Springs, Kansas, on the Oklahoma border. But the Daltons lost all credibility as law enforcers when Bob shot an Indian boy in the Cherokee community of Claremore during the spring of 1890. The slayer claimed it was a case of mistaken identity. Whatever the truth, the two territories had had enough of the three Daltons.

Oklahoma installed its first territorial government during May 1890. By the last day of June, the boys had laid down their badges. Miss Florence Quick, Bob's replacement for shallow Minnie Johnson, was in Silver City, New Mexico. A tough town it was, having known the likes of Wyatt Earp, Billy the Kid, John Selman, Roy Bean, and other such gentry of the gun. Riding herd over the citizens, good, bad, and mostly in between, was Marshal Ben Canty, an old Missouri neighbor who claimed Flo and the Daltons as longtime friends.

Under the aura of a New Mexico lawman's badge was organized Oklahoma Territory's worst gang of outlaws. Three other men besides that equal number of Daltons made up the original nucleus of the bunch. These were George Bitter Creek Newcomb; Blackface Charley Bryant, a deadly marksman, so called because his cheeks were smudged with powder burns from Texas gunfights; and Bill McElhanie, who'd soon get cold feet and return to his sister in Arkansas.

Eugenia Moore was the name by which Emmett Dalton identified Flo Quick in his work, *When the Daltons Rode,* written with Jack Jungmeyer in 1931. This was also the name she may have used in Silver City. Wandering women of dubious callings very often wear many and variable monikers.

Emmett described her as "the intelligence bureau" of the gang. She knew the Morse telegraph code from chummy friendships with local operators. She learned the track signal system governing the passage of trains. She could pose as a magazine writer, thereby getting facts about arrivals, departures, and what money shipments the express cars might be carrying. She picked up warnings and rumors disseminated by telegraph or word of mouth about bandits. All of these rumors got back to the boys in their concealed dugout rendezvous on Jim Riley's ranch near Taloga, Oklahoma.

But she was not "frail." She was not slowly dying from "an encroaching malady," despite Emmett's pitiful accounts. Underneath her gracious manners she was hard as nails and prickly as cactus.

Flo was twenty-two when she threw in with the gang. Bob, its top hand, was twenty. She sided her man and helped him even if it meant side amours to his advantage—behavior for which he did not rebuke her.

Guthrie again became her residence and her main listening post. From this busy little town she rode mile upon mile, time after time, to contact the bunch at the dugout or to meet with Bob at some spot arranged for in advance. Woodward, Oklahoma, was one such place; Dover another. Yet underneath it all she looked forward to a home with children and Bob, maybe settled down to lucrative ranching, for as Emmett truthfully remarked: "If on the other hand, Bob was to be backed into a desperate corner, Eugenia would back into it with him. That was the kind of woman she was—'Our country, may she always be right, but our country right or wrong.' " Flo had merely substituted "my man" for "our country, right or wrong."

Marriage and resettlement was on Flo's mind when the gang pulled its first train robbery at Whorton, Oklahoma, on May 19, 1891. Flo, Bob, and the other two Daltons looked forward to grabbing $50,000 in loot from the safe of a Santa Fe express train. That sum they figured would take them all to South America, where land was cheap. They probably got the idea from the previous flight of the Butch Cassidy gang to Bolivia.

Florence had carefully cased the station and the tracks in the little town. This time, disguised as a man, she had secured the necessary information about arrival and departure of the train from the naïve local express agent. Flo learned that the ensemble on wheels would be carrying a large shipment of bills and "solid" money from a bank in Kansas City to another in Guthrie. Then she contacted Bob and the rest before herself spurring back to the gang's sympathizers living near the capital.

The three resident Dalton brothers plus Blackface Charley Bryant and Bitter Creek Newcomb had holed up meantime at Bitter Creek's homestead claim in Ingalls, near Guthrie. Bill and Grat Dalton were awaiting trial on possibly false charges of train robbery in California. Flo managed interim visits to Bob. They were jubilant over the outcome of migration money from what they were already calling "the honeymoon holdup."

The robbery came off as planned with Florence, dreaming of roses and a bridal gown, anxiously waiting word at the home of a friend. But the honeymoon added up to no more than sour disappointment. The loot: a bag containing canceled waybills, discarded telegrams, and other waste papers. Not even a single dollar bill was to be found in the mess. Besides, a smaller package with but $500 in greenbacks. On the divvy, each of the four bandits would receive only $125 apiece. Not enough to go off honeymooning to South America.

Making it worse, Blackface Charley, just to satisfy blood lust, had shot and killed the young station agent. Shocked witnesses were able to identify him by name. Now he would be hunted as the murderer, the Daltons as his accomplices.

Florence Quick was an unhappy lady.

In advance of the robbery, the hard girl had set up an advance hideout at the homestead of a sorry character named Ol Yountis. He lived on Beaver Creek near a settlement of hardworking Missouri émigrés. Flo promised unpalatable Mr. Yountis certain favors, never rendered, if he would give the bandits temporary refuge on their way back to their permanent headquarters at the Riley ranch.

Within a couple of days some upright ex-Missourians spotted the quartet hiding in the wods near the Yountis farm. They pursued the desperadoes to a pair of small hills called Twin Mounds. A furious battle followed. Two settlers—William Starmer and William Thompson—lay dead on the ground. The gang sped back to the dugout refuge on Jim Riley's spread.

Three murders in one week, all chargeable to the thieving Dalton gang. Marshals mobilized; country sheriffs began displaying reward posters in their offices; posses, never finding their quarry, set forth. The Daltons kept their main refuge provided by Riley, but shifted as necessity required. Gradually, with Flo's help, they developed a chain of hideouts, working, as Emmett put it, under the theory that if one place was discovered, "they would have another in which to move."

During the summer a dazzling woman thought to be a rich divorcee set up housekeeping at a rented house in Kingfisher County northeast of Oklahoma City. Nearby lived the Dalton family, who had left Kansas and returned to old stamping grounds at the time of the 1889 homestead run.

The woman gave her name as Daisy Bryant. She was actually Florence Quick, living under still another name with money acquired probably from prostitution or horse theft. Dalton sympathizers, and there were many among calloused farmers, whispered that she was actually the sister of Blackface Charley Bryant, wanted for helping gang members steal and kill. Charley, ailing, it is said from syphilis, was holed up in a secluded cow camp. But others, recognizing Bob Dalton, who had been seen near the house, informed tough marshal Ed Short wanting to make the acquaintance of Mr. Bryant.

Short caught Bryant at a hotel in Hennessy near Kingfisher. He loaded him on a train bound for Wichita, Kansas, where the bad man was expected to stand trial. He and Short killed each other in the baggage coach as the powder-scorched Texan tried escaping.

Four men were now dead from Dalton-connected slayings. Bob and Flo fled Kingfisher County. But Florence was still dreaming of marriage and money—enough money, anyhow, to float a try at marital bliss. The brothers fled to the Riley ranch hideout. Bob's fiancée, reverting to the handy brand of Tom King, went back to stealing horses.

It is said that she became the "banker" for the infamous, often-insolvent Dalton bunch, which now included Charley Pierce also, run out of his native Missouri; Bill Doolin, destined to rank next to the Daltons in historical immortality; Dick Broadwell, renegade son of a Kansas judge; and Bill Powers, on whom biographical material is scant.

In one of her other guises, Florence would be Eugenia Moore, self-styled magazine writer pretending to gather information for articles on railroading. Often railroad officials would tell her somber tales about the Daltons, the "writer" pursing her sensuous lips in shocked dismay.

Meanwhile Grat Dalton was convicted of the train-robbing charge in California. He escaped and fled to Oklahoma after a bleak stay on an icy mountain range. Bill Dalton was acquitted but was ruined financially and personally by the whole sensational episode.

Bill, disliked by Flo, also came back to fool around in real estate and to act as the gang's outside man, receiving a cut on each job that he helped them plan. Once more Bob and his girl planned matrimony, then flight with a big stake to some South American country—this time to Argentina.

After the next job the two planned to meet in Tampa, Florida. Emmett and Grat would follow. Bill thought he'd do better by skinning nesters out of their claims in Oklahoma. Besides, he felt the whole project was so much hokum.

Bob and Flo never got to Tampa. Neither did Grat and Emmett. Somehow Marshal Chris Madsen had heard of their dream venture. From what Flo learned through counterintelligence, he had the Florida port staked out, intending to grab the gang. So Flo consoled herself by buzzing around in Latin vaquero garb: shiny leather chaps, a high-peaked sombrero, silver-plated boots, and a flowery decorated *camisa*, or shirt. Today she could have passed for a professional rodeo artist. But now she was the queen of the country's most feared outlaw combine, glorying in her majesty. Meantime, she had staked out another haul for her admirers.

September 15, 1891. The place: an unguarded railroad flag stop at Leiliaetta in the Oklahoma cotton belt. Florence, from a previous flirtation with the station agent, had learned that an express train would be carrying proceeds from cotton crop sales to banks in Waco and Houston, Texas. Shortly after sunset the train halted to take on a few passengers. Seven men, led by Bob and Emmett, plundered it.

The sum was likely about $10,000, though Bob would always claim that it was $19,000. Grat was still en route from California, so he did not participate. The two brothers present gave their helpers only $200 apiece, then divided the remainder—about $8,500—between themselves. When the help protested, the partners announced they they were dissolving the business. Bob and Emmett knew the boys would be back when they whistled.

Emmett Dalton returned to interim cowpunching for Jim Riley. Bill Dalton was still living an outwardly respectable life as a realtor of sorts while keeping his brothers posted on developments that might affect them.

Flo Quick was still pining for domesticity. Bob went along with his woman but felt that they'd better try it in Texas, where there were no charge against the Daltons. Bill Powers, stealing horses under the alias of Tom Evans, helped them find a comfortable-enough house in Greer County, a remote section of the thinly settled Texas panhandle.

The isolated county was seldom troubled by visits of the ubiquitous Texas Rangers. It had more prairie dogs than people. It lay right next to Oklahoma, which would eventually detach it from Texas in a boundary feud decided by the U.S. Supreme Court. Out there in that land of sage and mesquite a pair of lovebirds found a perch.

It was the nearest thing to a home of their own that the couple would ever experience. As Mr. and Mrs. Boyd they were known to their few neighbors. Necessary merchandise for housekeeping was shipped to them by wagon freight from Fort Worth, Texas.

A Guthrie businessman named Mundy with whom she shacked up for varying periods may have unwittingly put up the money for Flo's love nest. Something of an oaf, Mundy always forgave her for her absences and didn't ask too sharp questions when she returned. Of course, her side connection meant that her adored Bob would always have spending money—within reason.

Florence sewed up counterpanes for bedspreads, cut and hemmed cloth for towels, made curtains of muslin with lace. My, my, what a contented lady she was.

But to keep in practice, she now and then stole a remuda of horses, to be resold in Texas border places like Vernon and Wellington. Her partners in these ventures: Powers, calling himself Evans and Dick Broadwell, known as Texas Jack.

Side by side, saddle to saddle, the larcenous lovers, Bob and Flo, rode. They picked wildflowers for the vases that Flo had brought from Guthrie. They potshot jackrabbits for their table and sometimes slew an antelope with one of Bob's rifles.

Their rawhide idyll lasted six months. But Bob got impatient with too much of the settled life. Besides, their funds were running low. Then they started realizing that what they had couldn't last forever. Much against her will, Florence prepared herself for another move.

About that time, Grat, looking woolly as a bear, smelling like a raccoon, arrived back in Oklahoma. In all, he had covered fifteen hundred miles before rejoining Emmett on the Riley ranch.

The word went out to the scattered gang. The Dalton firm would soon be back in business. Grat's return was a major boost to morale. A lucrative rail party was needed to celebrate.

A family council was held at the dugout. Later the rest of the gang started showing up at the glorified hole. A spot for a homecoming holdup was selected to honor Grat.

Red Rock, "capital" of the diminutive Otoe Indian Nation in northwest Oklahoma. Many of its members were friendly toward the Daltons, who sometimes dispensed small gifts of money or whiskey. Dense thickets made it convenient as a refuge from pursuers. Besides, the small nation was just forty miles south of Kansas. In that virtuous state the Daltons had partially grown up. But there were no criminal charges listed on their otherwise dubious records.

During the last week of May 1892, Bob and Flo left their comfortable home in Texas. Everything remained just as it had been, because they hoped to return at least temporarily. Moreover, few people on the Western frontier ever locked their doors. Flo had objected to the prospect of another wearying move, but Bob had dangled an alluring hope before her . . . that they would relocate in Mexico, buy a hacienda from the proceeds of the expected big haul at Red Rock, raise cattle and raise kids.

Florence went to Guthrie to catch up on her romantic obligations to Mr. Mundy. That affluent gent was showing signs of being less generous toward his precious wench. She needed, for Bob's sake, to placate her "banker."

Plans went forward in the dugout for that pending business at Red Rock. On the night of June 1, 1892, eight men stopped a Santa Fe passenger train. Bob Dalton, as usual, was in command. Seconding him were Emmett and Grat, exulting at pulling off his first train robbery for real. Five other bandits completed the pack—Bill Doolin, managing to conceal his usual dislike for Bob; Dick Broadwell; Bitter Creek Newcomb; Charley Pierce; and Bill Powers.

Eight men all told—together raising more hell on the rails than any combination since the James–Younger gang, now shattered with the death of Jesse and the imprisonment of Cole.

The outlaws reined their horses in a grove of trees. They boarded the coach after a quarter-hour, no-casualty battle with the guards. But the take was no more than $4,000 or $5,500 instead of the huge sum anticipated by Florence and Robert.

Bob's share would probably be no more than $1,900. Not even enough for a down payment on a ranch in Mexico.

Miss Quick cussed a little and cried a lot when she got the news. By items in the *Guthrie Leader*, plus grapevine reports transmitted by realtor Bill Dalton, posses were moving out in all directions. One such group was led by U.S. Marshal Ransom Payne, who had been aboard the train robbed by the gang at Whorton, but had jumped off and hidden in the bushes along the tracks.

Payne now needed to cleanse his blemished reputation. Moreover, as a federal officer, he could make arrests anywhere regardless of state or territorial boundaries. Most important, he had with him armed badge wearers bolstering his courage.

Living in Texas was no longer any protection for that

outlaw couple. Certainly not that part of Texas just some strips of dirt away from Oklahoma. By weight of logic, Payne was bound to make a descent on Greer County.

Bob and Flo managed a meeting in the then predominantly black community of Dover. Sorrowfully they agreed that their comfortable home with all its fixings would have to be abandoned. After those months of domestic bliss, Bob would once more have to "go on the scout," as outlaw flight was called. For the present, Florence would return to Guthrie to squeeze whatever could still be extracted from Mr. Mundy.

Meantime, that pillar of commerce was increasingly resistant to doles of cash requested by his lady for "donations" or visits to "sick relatives" or for the expensive things she kept ordering from Sears, Roebuck in Chicago. Why, he'd been perfectly hateful the last time she'd wheedled him for a thousand.

Payne, less blundering than usual, found the Greer County love nest. But the birds had flown, not to return.

Cooking utensils still hung on the kitchen walls. Beds were neatly made. Florence's fine mail-order negligees still hung in closets.

The few neighbors could give no accounting of the couple. Texas Rangers promised to look for them, but didn't hurry about doing it. They had enough problems with Panhandle fence cutters and Rio Grande rustlers. Let Oklahoma scoop up its own *mal hombres*.

The chase continued. The Dalton gang remained uncaught. Mr. Mundy tightened his purse strings. Meantime Bob needed still another thousand, Mundy flatly saying no.

But Flo tried to resolve that financial crisis of her man and involved no less a person than Guthrie's city marshal, Ed Kelley. While the hunt for the Red Rock robbers was as its height, she visited Kelley in his office.

She said lightly, "I can have Bob Dalton in my house on ——" She mentioned a certain date. "And we'll split the big reward for that old boy."

Kelley was astonished. Throughout the territory, this

handsome hussy was regarded as Dalton's girlfriend, except by Mr. Mundy, who had chosen to keep his ears shut on the subject. The marshal thought that Florence had gotten jealous of Bob over some other woman and that the outlaw was willing to risk death or capture by squaring matters with her.

Catching or killing the gang ringleader would be a feather in any lawman's cap. So Kelley, who also liked the scent of money, agreed to the scheme with one proviso: that a check signed by the Santa Fe's general agent in Guthrie would be delivered to the woman only if Marshal Chris Madsen made a positive identification, dead or alive, of the purported Bob Dalton.

Kelley had never met any of the Daltons personally. Madsen, then out of town, knew them all.

Flo wiggled over to a nearby saloon. Soon she was ogling a foolish-looking youth named Alf Barber. He was easily coaxed to the house she shared in shaky tenure with Mundy. From across the street Marshal Kelley and three of his officers watched them enter.

The four converged on the house. The policemen checked their revolvers. Bob Dalton was a top gunman. It might require a tough fight to arrest him.

The gawky lad inside must have heard the sound of triggers being cocked. "Don't shoot," he shouted. "I surrender."

The lawmen rushed inside, .45s cocked. The young man started blubbering. Tears rolled down his cheeks. He made no protest when Marshal Kelley clamped handcuffs on him. The officers couldn't believe what they were seeing. Bob Dalton giving up like a no-account man stealing one of those no-account animals—a sheep.

"This is Mr. Dalton," Flo quickly proclaimed loudly. "Watch him or he'll kill all of you."

Too stunned to talk, the boy was marched to Logan County Jail. There he was booked as Robert Dalton and charged with complicity in the Red Rock train robbery. By order of Sheriff John Hixon he was placed under heavy guard.

At midnight Marshal Madsen was awakened from his

bed in a Winfield, Kansas, hotel. An employee handed him a telegram dated from Guthrie and reading: "BOB DALTON WAITING IN COUNTY JAIL. REWARD PAYMENT AWAITING YOUR IDENTIFICATION." Madsen postponed pressing legal business in Kansas and rushed back to Oklahoma. He laughed wryly when he saw the suspect brought before him in the jail at Guthrie.

"Boys," he addressed the officers gathered around him. "You've let yourself be hurrahed by Dalton's woman. Turn him loose."

Florence Quick was furious. She had been unable to talk the Santa Fe agent into giving her the promised reward check as soon as the youth had been arrested. Now, too, she was facing eviction.

Mr. Mundy had ordered her to leave his home without delay. Otherwise, he threatened to go before the county grand jury and incriminate her in a lot of horse thefts.

It was the first time that a man had ever kicked her out. Marshal Kelley, feeling humiliated by the bogus Dalton episode, followed her down a street and ordered her to be aboard the next train. It was likely the last time that she would ever see Oklahoma's small capital city.

She went to Woodward, which remembered her as a demure, apparently solvent, single lady named Eugenia Moore.

Bob Dalton managed to slip in and out to see her occasionally. Otherwise, while successfully dodging lawmen, he and his brothers frequented the gambling joints of two new railroad centers: Tulsa, Oklahoma, and Denison, Texas. The four Daltons, outwardly peaceful Bill included, all seemed to be leading charmed lives.

But luck was turning—and grim times lay ahead.

On July 15, 1892, the bunch stopped a Katy (Missouri, Kansas, and Oklahoma) express train at Adair in the Cherokee Nation. Suddenly unexpected gunfire spewed from a coal shed across the tracks. Inside the crude building, firing at the exposed bandits, were U.S. Deputy Marshal Sid Johnson of the Wichita, Kansas, federal court; Captain J. J. Kinney of the MK&T special detective force; Captain Charles Le Flore, commander of the Cherokee National Police; and a railroad guard named Ward.

The Dalton luck held. None of the bandits was injured in the fierce brief battle that followed. But Marshal Johnson was seriously wounded; Ward and Kinney sustained minor flesh wounds; Captain Le Flore's arm was burned by a bullet. But the worst casualties were two incidental ones.

Adair's two physicians—Youngblood and W. L. Goff—were sitting in the local drugstore when they were struck by bullets crashing through windows. Dr. Goff died a few hours later. According to Oklahoma legend, Dr. Youngblood never fully recovered. The eight desperadoes rode away after forcing express messenger George P. Williams to open the safe.

Their take was probably no more than $5,000, though Emmett would always claim boastfully that it was $17,-000. It was the gang's biggest haul so far.

But Florence Quick sensed that the attempted ambush of the bunch indicated one plain fact: lawmen had been tipped in advance about the Adair holdup, hence their presence at the coal shed. She was right: Madsen and the other marshals at Guthrie were developing a counterespionage system that made the single person of a wild young woman look puny.

Investigators posing as landseekers or drifting cowboys wandered rural Oklahoma picking up bits of information about the Daltons and people friendly to them. They made lists of "tickbirds"—meaning those who aided the outlaws with food, information, or shelter. Reward offers for capture or leads on the gang members were substantially increased. To know the Daltons became less glamorous and often risky.

Florence Quick sensed the drift. Time now for the Dalton business to be liquidated. Time to get out of the United States, so long as routes of escape were open, for the margin of flight was lowering with more and more law-abiding people migrating West. Flo felt that not much choice between countries was left. Old Mexico, relatively close, seemed to be the alternative.

She went back to Silver City, where Mexican land could be picked up for ridiculous prices in American money. In that New Mexico community she haggled and dickered for acreage across the border. Alas, she didn't even have enough cash for a binding down payment.

In his semifraudulent book, Emmett Dalton had her dying in Silver City, to Bob's great grief. In point of accuracy, she would outlive the man she loved so desperately. Now a new course was shaping up for the bandit brothers . . . a course of fate.

Coffeyville. That town where the Daltons had done their first killing—the grudge slaying of Charlie Montgomery—but where they were yet to stage a robbery, this to be their first on Kansas soil . . . hopefully two robberies: the holdups of two banks in one operation, something brand new in American outlaw history. And that doubleheader to be attempted by just five men: Bob, Emmett, and Grat Dalton, Bill Powers, and Dick Broadwell.

The Dalton gang was playing for high stakes with a short deck. The date of that monumental fiasco: October 5, 1892, a month before Democrat Grover Cleveland's election as President, brightening Democratic Oklahoma's hopes for admission into the Union. The plan: for the gang to loot the two banks, the take being maybe $100,000. Afterward by the planned strategy of Bob and Flo, a black cowpuncher who admired the Daltons would transport the gang, disguised as emigrants, west across the thinly settled Oklahoma panhandle to the far hills of New Mexico.

There Dick Broadwell and Bill Powers would be left to fend for themselves. The three Daltons and Florence would proceed to Old Mexico, where, with all that money, they could buy a handsome rancho and rustle all the starting cattle they needed from the American side of the Rio Grande. In time, maybe, Julia Johnson, Emmett's girlfriend, could be persuaded to join the ménage and slip across the border. Julia had no allergy to the outlaw life as such, but moving into a land of strange customs and language was something else again.

It was all such a sweet dream for that band of Oklahoma's worst criminals. But the Daltons had forgotten one vital fact: everybody in Coffeyville knew and remembered them, recognized them under silly masks worn by Bob, Emmett, and Grat. Broadwell and Powers chose not to enter disguised.

Nine-thirty A.M.: the five desperadoes entered the town square, walking after having hitched their horses to the back fence of a lot opening into an alley. The outlaws quickened their pace to a dogtrot as they neared a store owned by townsman Alex McKenna. Their clothes and their rifles were all new, like the saddles of their horses tied to the fence a few score yards away.

"The Daltons," McKenna shouted. "There go the Daltons."

"The Daltons." The cries went up and down the street. Bob and Emmett entered the First National Bank. Grat, Broadwell, and Powers invaded the Condon & Company Bank on the opposite side of the street.

Citizens intent on wiping out the gang poured into a hardware store and passed out guns shipped by federal marshals previously tipped to the intended raid.

For all the careful planning of Flo and Bob, the Dalton gang had walked into a trap—a trap set by a local gun club after the marshals in Guthrie had notified its president, John J. Kloeher, that the bandits might be expected during the first week in October.

On that day of blood and lead, the bandits collected more than $20,000 from the two banks. But they emerged to the spewing of bullets and the stifling smoke from gun barrels. "It looked like that everybody in Coffeyville was shooting at us," Emmett Dalton would recall years later. But four citizens would die in the battle.

Of the five bandits Emmett was the only survivor, and

he would be captured as a seriously wounded prisoner. Powers and Broadwell would be dead—as well as Grat and Flo's Bob. This after the desperadoes found that their passageway through the alley had been blocked during their absence by a horse-drawn oil tank. The money went back into the banks.

Somewhere in New Mexico, a tough girl waited for a man who would never return. There were no news or radio telecasts in those days when the phonograph was something wondrously new and the moving picture still to come.

Florence would have learned of her lover's death perhaps from wire-service stories in a newspaper. Or just as likely from one of the interconnected outlaw grapevines. From one or the other such source she would have read later of Emmett Dalton's conviction with a long sentence for his part in the Coffeyville fiasco.

But she herself would have hit boot hill before Emmett was pardoned after serving fourteen years, then returning to a society with which he had made his peace.

Seeking savage revenge upon that society, Florence Quick of so many side monikers tried organizing her own small gang of freebooters. It didn't last long and Flo didn't long survive the death of her Robert.

We do not know the exact date of her passing. Nor did another cousin, Roscoe D. Wallis, know when in 1963 he talked with Harold Preece about his spectacular relative.

She was still under twenty-five when she was buried somewhere apart from Bob, who lay interred with Grat at a cemetery in Coffeyville. Ironically, that holdup backfired because a bedraggled old saddle tramp had excelled her as an informant.

This character was being held in Guthrie jail on a bootlegging charge. Bob had refused him admission to the tightly knit Dalton gang, but he had overheard the boys mentioning their plans for Coffeyville while hanging around them.

So bucking for clemency, he had spilled to the marshals. From knowledge supplied by a drifter, the wheels had been set in motion to wipe out the bunch in all its sorry glamour.

All of this Miss Quick never knew. Nor had she ever realized her wish to bear just one more name: Mrs. Dalton.